Among the Risen

MAKENA SONG

Cover Art © 2024 Avadel Inc.

Map artist: Edwin Menzo from "Fantasy Map Shop"

Printed in the United States

Paperback ISBN 979-8-9937833-5-2

ACKNOWLEDGMENTS

First and foremost, I would like to thank my mother, Tina Song, who spent countless hours not only listening to my endless brainstorming sessions but also editing my fantasy novel from start to finish. Without her loving support, I wouldn't have been able to pursue the path of a full-time writer or publish my first novel!

Second, I would like to acknowledge my incredible friends, who have supported me from my first draft on Wattpad to my final publication on Amazon. Because of their heartwarming comments, I was able to push through to the end of the novel! During every instance of writer's block, they served as a major motivation to continue writing.

Third, I would like to thank a wonderful woman, Ivy Gilbert, who formatted this book! Not only is she an amazing adviser who has answered any and all of my questions, but she also is an inspirational author who has published many of her own books! Without her expert insight and patient soul, I wouldn't have been able to navigate this process so smoothly.

TABLE OF CONTENTS

BOOK II – AMONG THE RISEN

Among the Risen

BOOK II
The Fallen Realms Series

Talis Mountains

Bluewater ✪

Kingdom of Avrith

Acton

Twyndale

✪ Faeran

Shimmering Glades

Portacle Sea

Forest

Dark Lands

N
W   E
S

I

DEATHLY DREAMS

During his childhood, Lucian dreamed of death. Flashes of Remus's abuses left a mark in his memories. Life was a living hell. Most humans ponder how they will die, but he didn't. He knew *how* he was going to die. The only question was *when*. "Soon" was the answer he had formulated after his father broke more and more of his bones each day.

The concept of death, however, intrigued his youthful mind. He faced the threat of death daily, so the end wasn't frightening. What filled his curious mind was what death would be like. How did death affect his senses—his taste, his vision, his hearing, and his smell? He didn't care much about how death affected pain because he already knew.

Death was a release from pain.

In his lowest mental state, he envisioned death as a life form with a morbid personality, distinguishing scent, and metal scythe. In his mind, death was a complex creature with dual personalities: One, an emotionless soul retriever; two, a bloodthirsty tyrant seeking destruction. Appearance-wise, death had icy white hair and arctic blue eyes with a fitting black cloak wrapping around his imposing figure. He imagined the scent of death was bittersweet—a mixture of rotting corpses and blood-red roses.

Not the soothing fragrance of lavender.

Why did death smell like lavender then?

The overwhelming smell assaulted his senses. The numbness activated during his fall ceased as his conscious mind returned. He felt the weight of the fall crash against him all at once. Surges of pain shot through his body, causing his muscles to twitch. His mouth was dry as a desert, and his vocal cords burned like fire. His eyelids seemed glued shut, icky gunk cementing his eyelashes together.

Bleh!

Lucian managed to break through the gunk.

His eyes struggled to open, a periphery of dark-brown wooden walls greeting him because of his success.

Where am I? This doesn't look like the afterlife to me.

Blurry splotches of brown walls transformed into a

furnished, spacious bedroom. His eyes roamed the room as far as they could see since his neck wasn't cooperating yet.

Far-right in his vision, a snoozing man sat.

A strange wave of recognition washed over him, like during his first meetings with Aaron and Angelique. However, a nasty heat rose in his chest, and his head throbbed painfully, unlike the other two meetings. He couldn't recall who this man was. He had certainly never met him in this life. At least, he didn't think he had.

Looking closer at him, the man had pearly-white hair and a broader, muscular body. He appeared to be no older than his late forties. And while he didn't think this man was death, Lucian couldn't jump to any conclusions so soon.

The rhythmic rising and falling of the man's chest as he snored made Lucian less and less sure, as he imagined death didn't need to breathe or sleep.

His attire was also not death-like. The man wore a skintight, blue coat reaching down to his knees, a plain, white undershirt beneath it, and knee-high, weathered brown boots.

"Ahem!" He emphasized the word, a scratchy sound escaping his lips. He really needed water to clear the drought in his throat. When the man didn't budge, Lucian repeated, saying, *Ahem!* It worked after the fifth or sixth time.

The white-haired figure yawned, exaggerating a stretching motion with his limbs. His eyes fluttered open, immediately looking at the conscious Lucian, who stared blankly back at him. A pleased look crossed his face. He leisurely lifted himself off the chair, rising to his feet and walking over to where Lucian was lying.

"Looks like our guest is finally awake," the man said, with a gentle tone. "Better late than never, I suppose."

"Who..." Lucian struggled to speak. "...are you?"

The man crossed the distance between the chair and the bed within a few broad steps. "My apologies, my name is Leon Alastair. I am Avrith's most renowned locksmith."

"You're..." he struggled to say, "...not death?"

In a playful tone, the man teased, "I don't look that old, do I?"

His jest didn't elicit an immediate response. Lucian stared blankly at him and then sincerely shook his head, responding, "*No.*"

"I guess that's enough silly talk," Leon apologized, slightly bowing his head. "For starters, you probably would like to know what happened to you...after the fall?"

Lucian's brows furrowed, and his neutral expression turned into a frown with the remembrance of Aaron's betrayal. He nodded his head as carefully as possible. His muscles still resisted any complex motions. Even sitting up felt like an impossible task.

Leon crossed the room once more to retrieve the chair, dragging it closer to where Lucian was. "This may take a while, so I might as well sit down," the man said, mostly to himself. "Do you remember Eva wanting Aaron to deliver a package to Avrith—to me?"

Lucian nodded as his pale blue eyes roamed over to his belongings, which lay on a nearby table. He had completely forgotten about them. All of his items seemed to be accounted for: Master Felix's notebook and scepter, Eva's ring, Aaron's note and rock, his useless sword, Ignis, and Melinda's Credit Slip from Caelum. He then spotted an ornate, ceramic bowl of essential oils.

So that's where the lavender smell was coming from...

His gaze flicked over and lingered on one specific item. Leon caught onto the silent message. Both of their eyes rested on Eva's ring, reminding Lucian of her last request.

Leon returned his gaze to Lucian.

"You seem to be focused on her ring, maybe even confused. Did something happen to Eva?" Leon questioned.

Lucian lowered his head in despair.

"Everyone has left you in the dark about your purpose and mission," Leon stated, guiltily, "but I want you to know the truth. To begin with, the package Aaron originally intended to deliver wasn't a physical item. It was *you*."

"Aaron," Lucian said with spite, in between coughs.

"He..." He clamped his mouth shut. He wasn't sure that he could trust this man, so he reverted to silence.

Scratching his head, Leon explained, "As for the fall, my adopted daughter, Seraphina, found you unconscious on the riverbank near The Talis Mountains. She was out retrieving herbs for a certain medicine. I'm shocked that you survived the fall. Your body miraculously missed the rocks and landed in the river. You truly are beloved by the gods."

Lucian scoffed at the mention of the gods.

"Now that you're awake, we must get to work immediately," he explained. "The Terras Empire's political situation has escalated over the past year to the point of threatening a global war."

A look of suspicion formed on Lucian's face. Leon interpreted the expression correctly and said, "If I wanted you dead, then I would've had numerous opportunities to kill you when you were lying in a coma. For example, I could've told Seraphina to leave you bleeding on the riverbank, refused to let Seraphina care for you over the past few months, or even allowed that nasty affliction to eat you until you were nothing but a skeleton. Be thankful to Seraphina. She invested so much time in caring for your wounds and condition, even trekking to the top of The Talis Mountains to retrieve the necessary medicinal herbs."

Over the past few months? Lucian squirmed. *What is he talking about? What affliction?*

Fear overtook pain.

He forcibly moved his body, the pain shooting through his limbs like arrows striking his flesh. Leon hurriedly assisted Lucian to a seated position, propping a pillow behind his back.

"Sorry, I shouldn't have mentioned that part yet," Leon apologized again. "You were near death when we found you. You lost so much blood, but you were breathing. The gods protected you. You should thank whatever— or, whoever—was protecting you. It did more than just save your life; it stopped the mana-devouring curse on your body. Without its assistance, you would've been dead within a day."

"What...curse?"

"See for yourself."

Lucian anxiously peeked under his shirt. The speck of blue that he had found on his chest in The Tribal Nations had grossly expanded across his torso. It looked like pulsating veins, spreading almost down to his waistline. He reflexively shuddered in shock.

"The curse has progressed quite far, but now that we know it's there, we can treat it," Leon explained. "For now, try to take it easy."

"Angelique Maroon," Lucian recalled. "I think she was the one who cursed me."

"Ahhh," he said, brows rising like he recognized the name. "Even for a skilled Mage like her, I don't think she's capable of such a curse."

"What...do...you...mean?"

"Take my word for it," Leon started to say, "this curse has a lot more to it than you'd think. Even so, we have ways to fix the problem at the root."

"Where...is...Aaron?" Lucian abruptly changed the subject, squeaking out the words through gritted teeth. "That...traitor..."

"About the same time that we found you half-dead on the riverbank, Aaron completely vanished. I'm of the opinion that these two incidents aren't coincidental. We desperately need you to fulfill your destiny now more than ever, Lucian. I beg of you, please save Gaia."

All of the talking made Lucian's throat even more sore.

"Water," he pleaded, starting to wheeze.

Leon reached over to the nearest table, where Lucian's items and a conveniently placed pitcher of water sat. Pouring the water into a ceramic cup, Leon returned to his side. Since Lucian couldn't hold the cup without shaking, Leon carefully held on to the cup for him, positioning it by his lips and quenching his thirst.

Thank the gods, Lucian sighed in relief. *Water tastes better than I remember.*

"I should let you rest," Leon said. "You must have a lot on your mind after our chat, so I want to give you time to recover physically and emotionally. Seraphina will arrive later to tend to your wounds."

A heavy haze filled his mental space. Lucian slept within a minute of Leon leaving the room. His lingering feelings before dozing off were a contradictory mix of relief and disappointment—a genuine relief that he was still alive, as well as a deep-seated disappointment that he had to relive these memories repeatedly.

He fell into an uneasy sleep.

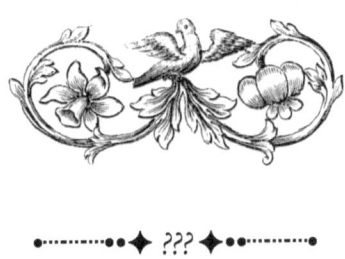

•············••✦ *???* ✦••············•

Scenes of his former friend's betrayal plagued his dreams, turning them into nightmares. His mind wouldn't release him from this endless hell. Trapped in an unbreakable mental cell, he was tortured by the past. He screamed with all of his might, yet the images wouldn't stop haunting him. No number of his father's beatings even came close to the mental exhaustion and agony that he currently felt.

He gave up on fighting the past. He extinguished the flames of rage consuming his heart. He watched with apathy, letting his heart harden and surround itself with a steel encasement. That was when the observer revealed himself.

A figure clothed in all black with a concealing hood motioned for him to follow. A wry smile played on the stranger's lips.

Rising to his feet after falling, Lucian staggered slowly after him. Crossing an ominous-looking bridge, a thick mist enclosed the area around him. Why was he so willing to follow the stranger? Even he didn't know. He just did as his body told him to do.

Walking on the path to an unknown destination, Lucian passed by several familiar structures. He first encountered the buildings of Faeran, Korakk, and then Lunaris. Not a living soul was in sight, so he assumed that the town was desolate.

But that wasn't the case.

Laughter and merry voices came from within the building. The sounds were cheerful, not distorted or twisted. Somehow, the voices managed to travel through the mist, even though Lucian's vision was obscured.

Soon enough, the mysterious figure disappeared into the distance.

When the mist cleared further down the road, Lucian wished he had never followed the figure. Laughter turned to cries, happiness turned to sadness, and life turned to death. His apathetic lens on life broke in a matter of seconds.

He was back in Caelum.

The streets were uprooted, the houses were destroyed, and the people were gone. Off in the distance, where The Heavenly Pillars were, a bright light beamed into the sky. None of this mattered to him. Why would he care about the people who openly condemned him? And then he remembered her, the only one he truly cared about in Caelum.

"Rosalie!" he yelled.

"Lucian..." A voice beckoned. "Lucian...come here. Come to me...."

Where was that voice coming from?

He had a gut feeling where it was, but he wasn't certain. Entering a few houses and public buildings, his search bore no fruit. He ultimately decided to follow his gut. The bright stream of light on the outskirts of the village was no mere coincidence. His nightmare was trying to tell him something.

Deep down, he knew what was to come; after all,

nothing good comes from nightmares—nothing good at all.

Upon approaching The Heavenly Pillars, he noticed tiny black specks lying all around the base. He squinted his eyes, thinking they were only pieces of rubble. His feet crossed the long distance, padding against the hard, rocky surface.

Reaching the pillars, he realized that he was wrong. His face flushed pale. His stomach gurgled in disgust. He was about to vomit.

They weren't rubble at all...

They were *corpses*.

A wave of grief washed over him. Scanning over the bodies, he recognized many familiar faces. Neighbors, peers, Mages, and Elders were mere mountains of unmoving flesh. Even so, he hurriedly searched for his family, specifically Rosalie. Eventually, he found Remus, who had a dagger wedged in his chest, and Melinda, whose body was riddled with disease. He winced at the sight of them.

But where was Rosalie?

"Lucian!" A girl's voice shrieked. "Help me!"

Lucian's head turned to look at his weeping sister. Atop the ruins of The Heavenly Pillars, Rosalie was held captive by a masked figure. She squirmed, trying to break free but to no avail. The cloaked figure wasn't the same one who had guided him into Caelum. This figure had a knife pressed against Rosalie's throat. Her usually gentle expression was warped with fear.

"Let her go!" Lucian cried. "Let my sister go!"

He raced toward the two at full speed. But as always, he was too late. The knife slit her throat, and his world crumbled beneath him. The same wind that exposed Aaron's betrayal revealed the identity of the cloaked figure. Just like the nightmare that he had experienced before, the figure was Lucian himself. A devilish grin flashed on the figure's face.

"What have you done!" Lucian screamed.

"No," the figure cackled, throwing Rosalie's body amongst the other corpses. "What have **you** done?"

Thin, icy fingers wrapped around his shoulder. Something ominous stood behind him out of view. It said to him in a voice that it knew would haunt him, "You should've died when you had the chance, Lucian."

With a forceful push, he fell into a sea of darkness.

2

CITY OF SORCERY

 *Avrith*

I t was love at first sight... The object of his affection had a plump, velvety body. The skin looked silky and succulent, emitting a sweet aroma of honey and hibiscus. He licked his dry, cracked lips, drool pooling in his mouth. His stomach gurgled greedily.

A mesmerizing morsel sat before him. Steam radiated off the surface. He impatiently reached out to grasp it—his most desired object—the roasted chicken. He reached out to touch the fine meat when his hand was stopped.

"Not yet," a firm voice said, gently stalling his hand from moving. "I'm not done preparing the meal. Be patient."

After watching the chicken for a few more seconds,

Lucian finally acknowledged the cook. A sixteen-year-old girl stood before him, holding a confident posture with her shoulders straightened and her gaze unshaken. Wavy, scarlet hair went past her shoulders, reaching mid-length down her back. A pair of maroon eyes interlocked with his blue ones.

Not so subtly, he observed her attire. She wore a puffy, white shirt with a pair of gray pants reaching her ankles. A light purple bodice hugged her chest, extra fabric reaching down a few inches from her thighs held together by a long, brown belt. Most striking was the royal-blue cloak she wore.

"Where..." Lucian started to ask her.

"...are you?" Seraphina finished his question. "We're in Leon's locksmith shop, The Broken Latch."

The shop's name seemed strangely familiar; however, that thought immediately escaped his mind as his stomach gurgled with hunger.

"Hungry," he said, curtly.

"Fine," she replied. "I bet you don't even know my name, and you still boss me around like a maidservant."

"Seraphina."

She blushed slightly while saying, "Never mind, then."

From the royal-blue cloak, she pulled out a wooden wand. Waving it gently in the air, she recited a string of ancient words. She approached the food platter, lightly tapping his meal with the wand. A light wind whirled around the affected area, the savory chicken turning into a brown pile of mush.

"Why...!" he whined.

Letting out a long sigh, Seraphina explained, "You can barely speak. How in Gaia's name are you going to eat without some form of assistance? You've been in a coma for the past few months. Your stomach isn't ready for solid foods, so be patient. Eat your mush and stop complaining. It'll taste the same, either way."

Lucian's stomach now gurgled for another reason...in disgust. His delectable chicken had been transformed into an unsavory mess. Reluctantly, he scooped up the mush with a metal spoon. He eyed it doubtfully. However, his empty stomach took precedence. He braved the awful appearance and shoved the bits of brown mush into his mouth.

As Lucian was about to shove the spoon back into his mouth, Seraphina exclaimed, "What did I just tell you? Slow down!"

Before she could steal the spoon, Lucian *slowly* took his next bite.

Much to his surprise, the mush was edible. While the meal was bland in appearance, the taste remained unchanged from the transformation. The chicken was just as juicy, tender, and scrumptious as Lucian dreamed it would be.

Honestly, magic confused him.

"See, I told you it wasn't *that* bad," Seraphina said, proudly. "Now, let's move on to the next part of your daily routine."

Lucian raised one eyebrow in confusion while thinking, *And what is that?*

Seraphina easily guessed Lucian's internal thoughts.

She smiled while saying, "Rehab."

•••••••••◆ *Avrith* ◆••••••••

AFTER TWO WEEKS OF GRUELING REHAB, LUCIAN was finally ready to move on to the next stage: an extended walk.

"I think it's time we get some fresh air. Leon thought you might enjoy a tour, depending upon your condition," Seraphina said.

He carefully slid off the bed to his feet, ascertaining that his body could handle his weight. He walked over to the mirror in the corner of the room. His legs were frail and thin. He looked up, staring into the reflective surface.

He wished that he never had.

Lucian's arms and legs were unhealthily skinny. The mana-limiting devices were hanging onto dear life and threatened to slide off at any moment. He suddenly wondered whether they were safe or not. While they faithfully completed their main functions, he couldn't ignore the fact that Aaron had given them to him. Even so, the devices hadn't negatively impacted his health.

At least, he hoped so.

Hanging over his torso was a loose, white tunic reaching down to his mid-thighs. Taking off his shirt, his ribs were nearly visible. His stomach was deflated like a popped balloon, and dark circles were engraved beneath his eyes. He looked like a specter.

As deathly as he appeared, he wasn't a skeleton due to the constant care from Seraphina's care and Aerus's protection. To be honest, he could've looked a lot worse.

Crossing to the other side of the room, Lucian slid on the dark blue tunic and a pair of white, ankle-length pants. Neatly folded beside the other garments was a pure-white cloth. He unfolded the cloth, revealing a new cloak for him to wear.

Ah, that's right, he recalled. *My old one was ripped when I fell off the cliff.*

Lucian felt almost relieved. He slung the cloak over his shoulders, tying the cloth in a bow tightly around his neck. He smoothed out the wrinkles and looked at his new attire in the mirror. Although pale and skinny, he found the outfit rather charming. The last item was a pair of knee-length boots—the same color as Leon's. He slid them on, tying the laces in a sturdy knot.

He then transferred the items back into his inner pockets. Eva's ring, Master Felix's notebook and scepter, and Aaron's note were placed snugly in the cloak's inner pocket.

Never knowing when he would need these items, he kept them close to his heart. As for the Credit Slip, however, he stuffed it casually into his pants pocket. He then grabbed onto Ignis, sheathing the sword in his hilt. Stubborn as usual, the sword refused to speak.

Next, he flipped through Master Felix's notebook, finding the page that mentioned the location of the remaining prophetic items: In Avrith, The Broken Latch was listed, which was the shop where he currently resided. Lucian knew from experience that coincidences didn't exist.

The girl's impatient voice rang throughout the shop, so he hurriedly shoved the notebook into the inner pocket with the rest of the items. Shoving several bites of the unfinished meal into his mouth, he hastily left the room.

Although Lucian had seen this view several times during his shorter rehab walks, he was still amazed at its design. Outside of his relatively small corner room was an expanse of locks and other metal trinkets lining the walls, scattered in heaps on the floor, and resting on the nearest bar table. Illumination crystals were fixed within glass niches on the wall, lighting up the darker store. The store itself was mostly made of wood. The floorboards eerily squeaked as he walked.

The Master of The Broken Latch, Leon Alastair, sat at the bar, fiddling with a defunct lock. Most intriguing about Leon's craft was that he didn't rely solely on magic. Rather, the man appeared to use other metal tools to deal with the broken pieces of the lock. He was so deep within his work that he seemed too focused to notice Lucian.

Or so he had thought.

"Seraphina is outside waiting for you," Leon said. "Walking around the town will be a good way to strengthen those unused legs. Don't get into too much trouble. Oh, and one more thing, if you want to learn more about the items in your cloak, the old library at The Academy is your best bet."

"Thanks..." Lucian said, reluctantly.

Leaving the shop, Lucian spotted Seraphina waiting in the center of the cobbled road. She was blankly staring into the sky. A light breeze blew through the street, her hair flickering like vibrant flames in the wind. She turned her gaze to him, smiled, and then they started the tour.

Lucian was blessed with a clear sky and a brilliant sun, letting the rays soak into his entire being. He was finally able to enjoy the splendors of the town. The town's architecture was a sight to behold—a very different beauty than the previous locations he had visited.

Sitting along the road were muddy-brown cottages constructed of earth stones and maple wood. All lined up in a row, there was little to no space for an animal, let alone a human, to squeeze between them. The road was formed from dark gray and rusty-brown cobblestones cemented in mortar. He was amazed at the distinct aura of the environment: A cozy and welcoming feeling emitted from the townspeople.

"Can you tell me the name of this town again?"

"Bluewater," she answered, unenthusiastically. "Bluewater of Avrith is a manufacturing town, which mass produces magical tools and weapons." She seemed to grimace at her own words.

"Is that a bad thing? Magical tools are in high demand, so the town should be prosperous, right?"

Seraphina's face scrunched up, and she scowled while saying, "Sure, the town is economically well off, but wealth corrupts people's minds. It clouds their judgment and exacerbates discrimination."

Watching the girl's reaction, Lucian cautiously asked, "Who do they discriminate against?"

"Mages," she responded, curtly. "Since Mages don't need to buy magical tools like Sorcerers do, their businesses are attacked by those who only want to line their pockets."

Lucian gulped down his words while thinking, *I better not tell anyone that I'm a Mage. I could get beaten, or worse, killed.*

"Are you a Mage?" he asked with a soft voice. "Is that why you despise them?"

She shook her head while saying, "Not me...but Leon is. Blackwater's main manufacturers are pressuring the Elders for an edict that would put every Mage out of business. I hate what they're trying to do to him. His customers are dwindling because of this ridiculous farce."

"Do you hate Sorcerers?"

"No," she denied. "What I hate are the manipulative manufacturers, not the Sorcerers. They are pawns too..."

Their conversation gradually died down. He didn't want to pry too much as the topic obviously aggravated her. To distract himself, he counted the magical shops on the way to wherever they were headed. Surely, her story made sense. In total, they passed fifteen magic shops by the time they reached their destination.

Almost too naturally, Seraphina covered her head with her hood mid-stride. Lucian followed suit, wondering why it was necessary. But he soon understood why.

A bustling marketplace stretched out before him. Tons of people filled the tight spaces allotted to each vendor. It was ten times busier than anything he had experienced in Caelum.

Seraphina seemed unfazed. She casually locked hands with him, dragging him into the chaos of the crowd. Other than during The Rebirth Festival, Lucian had never been in such a concentrated space filled with hundreds of people. It was extremely difficult to keep his hood in place. He had a sinking feeling that something terrible would happen if it were to fall off, even by accident.

Both Lucian and Seraphina held on to their hoods with their free hands. A look of determination swept across the girl's face. She successfully fought through the crowd. If it were only Lucian, he would've been swept up by the current.

The furthest corner of the marketplace was where Seraphina headed. He followed her line of sight, assuming that the tiny, weathered shop was her intended destination.

Approaching the shop, Lucian noticed an old granny sitting at the splintered counter. She had a welcoming yet disconcerting smile. Her eyes met Lucian's.

"Hey, why are we here?" he asked, nervously.

"You'll see," she replied.

Once they reached the estranged vendor, they stepped through a clear, indiscernible barrier. The old granny seen from the outside was nothing but a mere illusion. An entirely different vendor sat snuggly behind the barrier.

The vendor sat lazily on a wooden chair, leaning back and resting his feet on the counter. He nodded to Seraphina and seemed unfazed by Lucian, the newcomer.

"Grab what you need and go," the vendor said.

Seraphina approached a table lined with a variety of colored potions. She chose the potion that she needed and selected a different one for Lucian. She tossed the potion toward him, and he caught it in midair. Upon inspection, the potion had an amber hue. He tilted his head to the side while asking, "What am I supposed to do with this?"

"Drink it," the vendor instructed.

Asking Seraphina was useless since she popped off the cork of her potion and chugged it down without a second thought. The potion must've been bitter because she winced after swallowing the contents. He pondered the difference between the two potions. Her potion was a rosy-pink color and tasted bitter. He braced himself for the potion's gross flavor. In one swift gulp, he downed the watery contents, instantly feeling its effects.

Ugh!

He fell to the ground with a *thump*. His heart threatened to fail, while his mind violently reacted to the potion.

Seraphina ran over to him, not saying a word. She whipped out her wand, tapping the tip on his bracelets and anklets.

They fell off, smacking the ground. After a few seconds, Lucian gradually regained his senses.

"What did you do? What was that potion?"

Seraphina bent down while explaining, "The potion fulfills the same purpose as those bracelets and anklets, except that it's an internal regulator rather than an external one. Its effects are also more potent and last longer."

Coughing out the icky taste in his mouth, he asked, "Then, why did you drink a different potion?" He was openly skeptical of her actions.

She seemed to eye the vendor, who pretended not to listen. She then said, sourly, "I've always had a mana deficiency, so the potion that I drank was to boost my body's natural mana production. How ironic, right? A person with my hair color needs a mana boost. Isn't it laughable?"

"What do you mean?"

"People with red hair are thought to have the most mana," she explained. "Blonde-haired people come next..."

"I didn't know that..." he responded.

Seraphina regained her composure. She suddenly stood up, stifling her feelings. She grabbed onto Lucian's arm, helping him to stand. She nodded to the vendor and then left with Lucian in tow. His devices, which were magically torn off, vanished when he looked back. Maybe Seraphina had whooshed them away, or maybe they were discarded. Either way, if he didn't need them to control his mana, then they weren't his concern anymore.

Once they were outside the town square, Seraphina abruptly stopped. She seemed sad, a wave of regret washing over her face. She kept trying to say something to him.

"Are you okay...?" he asked. "Should we continue the tour another time?"

"No." She shook her head. "I promised Leon to bring you to The Academy."

"Why is it so important that I visit The Academy?" Lucian asked. "Is something *really* there, or is it just another wild goose chase? All I want are answers..."

Seraphina released his hand while saying, "Even I don't know if they're the answers that you're seeking."

"Then, why?"

"How can you find answers if you refuse to even try?" she asked, seriously.

"Why should I trust you?" he asked with a caustic tone, wary of her words. "How can I know that you won't betray me like *he* did?"

"I guess saving you wasn't enough to earn your trust," Seraphina stated, sadly. "Even so, Leon thinks The Academy will reveal something to you."

"Reveal what?"

"The reason you were chosen."

3

THE ACADEMY (PART 1)

"Curse the gods!" Sacrilege upon sacrilege spilled out of Seraphina's mouth. Spitting contemptuous words while haphazardly waving her wand skyward and earthward seemed not to satiate her frustrations. Every failed incantation drove the girl further into her own little world.

At one point, her sanity snapped, and she proceeded to punch the obstruction so hard that her knuckles began to bleed. It was then that Lucian had lost hope in his tour guide.

He watched the pitiful events with a tinge of disappointment but mostly disassociation. Since Seraphina was too far gone, he resorted to whistling, yawning, and fiddling with his fingers to pass the idle time. He offered to help her endeavors, but she resolutely refused.

After the fiery-haired youth had completely exhausted her mana, she huffed, puffed, and then yelled, "Why can't I break this stupid thing!"

"So unladylike," he mumbled in between sighs. "Can I make an attempt?"

Seraphina defiantly puffed out her chest, crossing her arms and saying, "Sure, it's not like it'll budge."

It's just a simple barrier protecting a school. How hard can it be? He recalled the barrier surrounding Caelum.

The barrier maintained similar textures but separate properties from the one in his village. He rested his right hand on the slippery yet firm surface. He lightly knocked his knuckle on the barrier, confirming that it was as hard as concrete. He focused his mind, allowing the accumulating mana to flow through his body to the barrier. Just as he had practiced during his training in Faeran, he meticulously weaved and connected his mana to its surface.

"*Minuere*," he incanted.

Waves of mana rippled through the barrier, its form shifting from a concrete-like state to a soft, pliable state. From skyward to earthward, the barrier dissipated.

What lay beyond the barrier was their much-awaited destination: The Academy.

Seraphina stood speechless.

"Two hours and five minutes," Lucian muttered, "that's how long you took."

A blush of embarrassment reddened Seraphina's face, as she pouted and retorted, "I was just testing you! No need to thank me."

Lucian rolled his eyes.

"Anyway," she said, slowly regaining her confidence. "The Academy awaits!"

"Karma will inevitably find you," he stated, "if the truth isn't where you say it is."

"Haha!" she proclaimed. "O, you of little faith, have you no trust in me?"

He scowled while saying, "Trust is best earned. I'll *trust* you when you *show* me the truth."

An awkward silence ensued.

Since they were on the outskirts of The Academy's campus, the walk took around twenty minutes to reach the main entrance. An imposing black gate blocked their passage. Spikes sat atop the gate forewarning intruders, while ornate patterns were etched into the surface welcoming guests. A guard station sat to the left of the gate; however, it was left unoccupied. He pondered a good way to enter without destroying the gate.

"I got this," the girl said, triumphantly.

Swinging the wand skyward with one lavish motion, she chanted, "*Recludo!*"

The gate creaked wide open with a loud screech of metal scraping against cobblestone, unlocking its security latches and bolts. While the gate initially seemed a strong reinforcement, sorcery was even stronger. Seraphina proudly strode through the opened gate, while Lucian followed a safe distance behind. Since it was a school for magic, he could only imagine the tight security. If there were any hidden traps for intruders, then he wanted to be as far away as possible.

The sorceress seemed to speed up her pace, almost sprinting toward the destination. Thick forestry surrounded the cobblestone pathway on both sides, hiding the full expanse of The Academy's structure. Twigs and leaves lay motionless on the earth beneath the trees.

"Hey, where are you—"

His words fell flat.

In a single instant, the forestry cleared, and The Academy came into full view. Lucian didn't even acknowledge Seraphina as she started to blab about trivial things. He stood mesmerized at the entrance. The Academy towered dozens of someone's feet above him, a regal and elegant aura emitting from its form. Ivory-white arches supported the bottom floor, creating a passageway for students to walk. Each of the floors had navy-blue roofs and archways connecting to rectangular towers stationed on the right and left sides of the building.

Adjunct to the right corner, a spectacular clock tower stood. It had a wooden base and wall structure with glass windows stretching along its side, and the clock itself had a pearly, multicolored glass resting behind its hands.

The center of the building had a rectangular entrance with stained-glass windows held atop the structure. Past the archway, which served as the entrance, a huge, square-shaped building with four small watchtowers on the far edges, all with blue-colored tops, and sitting on each corner, lay behind it. From there, the main watchtower stood, its glass windows doubled in size from its smaller counterparts.

Lucian gawked at its larger-than-life features, while Seraphina lacked any noticeable reaction. She seemed to not care, briskly walking along the cobbled sidewalks. She only stopped when she noticed that he hadn't followed her.

With the snap of her fingers, she notified him that he was wasting time. He rolled his eyes again in response, clicking his tongue.

Way to ruin the mood.

After they passed through the entrance, a long stretch of corridors sprawled out into a bunch of different directions. Seraphina didn't seem fazed, as she chose a passageway leading northeast from their position. All he had to do was follow her and not get lost... Easy enough.

A few minutes later, they reached a ginormous room, which he assumed was the "old" library. There was absolutely nothing old about it. Master Felix's observatory and Rena's office paled in comparison to the floors and rows of books. The smell of old parchment wiggled its way into his nostrils, a unique but nostalgic experience.

Something felt off about the place, however.

"Hey, Seraphina," Lucian said, warily. "Where *is* everyone? I haven't seen a single soul."

Seraphina headed to the center of the room, flipping through a weathered brown book. Some of the pages were lined with a thick layer of dust. Each flip caused the dust to scatter and then settle back onto the weathered pages.

In between pages, she explained like a historian, "Due to the unrest between the manufacturers and the Mages, Bluewater decreed the temporary shutdown of The Academy until further notice. All of the students were told to vacate the premises effective immediately. Students from other kingdoms returned to their homes, and all of the professors relocated and found different occupations. A temporary shutdown is just a front since it's already been many years..."

"Exactly how long has it been shut down for?"

"Almost fifteen years," she said, "is what I heard from Leon."

"Was Leon affiliated with The Academy?"

"Uh-huh." She nodded. "Didn't he tell you?"

"Tell me what?"

"Leon and Felix were in the same year."

"Year?" Lucian tilted his head in confusion.

"They entered The Academy together, so they were placed into the same group of incoming students," she explained. "How can you not know something as simple as the sorting system? It's like you never went to school."

"Because I didn't," Lucian stated, bitterly.

Seraphina's face turned pale, and a deep sorrow filled her eyes.

With a stifled tone, she said, "I'm sorry. I didn't mean to..."

"What's done is done." He recited his mentor's words. "Can you show me what you're looking at?"

His question startled her, and she fumbled awkwardly while saying, "Yes, of course!"

She returned to flipping through the brown book, meticulously scanning each page. Deeper into the book, she seemed to find what she was searching for.

Lucian neared her, staring down at the contents. The girl pointed to a book's name near the bottom of the page and then slid her finger over to its location within the library.

"Myths and Legends: The History of the Primordial

Deities and Their Reincarnations," she read aloud. "Currently available, floor two, section A, row three."

A set of spiral staircases stretched to the very top of the library. They ascended the flight of stairs to the second floor. Seraphina led the way, smoothing her fingertips along the bindings of every book that she passed. Lucian refrained from touching the books since they seemed delicate, and he didn't like the thought of accidentally breaking their bindings.

One book, however, caught his eye.

"On the History of The Dark Lands," he read the title aloud. "Hey, Seraphina. What's *The Dark Lands*?"

Upon hearing the name, she charged toward him, not out of anger but out of excitement. Something seemed to well up inside of her, threatening to burst with the slightest trigger.

Consumed by her intrigue, she babbled while saying, "Good find, Lucian! The Dark Lands is a set of territories located in the southeast region of Gaia. Legend has it that these lands house thousands upon thousands of mythical creatures, ranging from Fairies to Goblins to Elves." Her eyes sparkled with an intense zeal for the subject.

"You mentioned 'legends' about The Dark Lands," he said. "Does that mean no one has actually been there?"

"Keen observation!" She squealed, continuing her history lesson. "Since they have geographical barriers such as mountains and seas on all sides, most adventurers are warded off. Although Avrith has the most direct access to The Dark Lands, no one dares to explore due to past incidents. Apparently, a long time ago, some soldiers and adventurers tried to travel to The Dark Land's residents, but the weather was too extreme to traverse the mountains and seas. There are rumors that an impenetrable barrier exists to prohibit intruders. Fascinating, right?"

Lucian shifted his gaze away from the book while saying, "Hmm, kind of sounds like a fairytale. So, where's the book on the Reincarnates?"

"Tsk, tsk," she voiced out each sound. "Patience is a virtue, Lucian. You should practice it sometimes."

"Humph." He rolled his eyes. "Says the one who struggled to break through the barrier. You're the least qualified person to talk to me about patience."

"You're gonna pay dearly for those words."

"Whatever you say."

By the time that they reached the book's location, a tense and deathly aura surrounded the two. One wrong move and the entire library would've been blown to pieces. At least the discovery of the book lessened the tension to some extent. Lucian retrieved the book from Seraphina's hands and sat down at one of the tables. His hands were shaking. He was apparently a lot more nervous than he had thought.

The book itself looked no different from any other stacked on the shelves. It was old-looking, brown-colored, and well-maintained. Most of it was filled with blacked-out portions or entire sections written in the ancient language.

He read through every section transcribed in the modern written language, as his reading skills in the ancient language were at best rudimentary.

His mentor didn't have enough time to teach him anything more than the basics. While the village's education system taught more complex forms of the ancient language, he didn't have access to them for obvious reasons.

Out of all the sections, one stood out. He couldn't tear his eyes away from it. Although worded like a child's bedtime story, the legend was scarily accurate in its details about Caelum's customs and Reincarnates' abilities.

A strange feeling consumed him.

He read word-for-word, "In Gaia's time of need, a hero shall arise from The Fallen Ones. Bestowed with the title, The Regulus, this hero shall be birthed only when all four of his attributes manifest and all four items are obtained. Then and only then shall The Risen be restored and Gaia released from her shackles. May the gods bless the one who shall save The Three Realms, The Almighty Regulus."

Lucian read the passage for a second time...

"Is this what you think I am?" he asked, shakily. "The Regulus?"

They locked their eyes.

"To be completely honest with you, Lucian," Seraphina stated, "I only know what I've been told second-hand, so I can't give you all of the answers that you want. However, I will tell you this: You were chosen because you fit the prophetic descriptions. Whether or not you truly are The Regulus, *they* still chose you. I hope that you will live up to *their* expectations."

Lucian put his forehead on the table and closed his eyes. His mind was spinning, and his stomach was performing backflips.

Think! Lucian, think! he internally proclaimed. *How could I possibly be The Regulus!?*

Connected images flashed into his head. He recalled a Reincarnate's four abilities: *Sense, Connection, Manipulation,* and *Interpretation.* To make sure, Lucian retrieved Master Felix's notebook, seeking out their definitions and manifestations.

He recounted the ways in which these abilities had revealed themselves during his travels. When had he manifested *Sense,* the gift of locating other Reincarnates? He thought back to the tingly, burning sensation when he had met Aaron, Angelique, and Leon.

No, no! They can't be fellow Reincarnates because they

would've told me... No, no, they wouldn't have. Aaron betrayed me, so everything about him is unknown, and Angelique never told me anything about herself. So, maybe...

He couldn't let himself fall into a mental rabbit hole, so he continued thinking about the other three abilities. *Connection*, the gift of knowledge, which was to know about one's past life or another's, was far-fetched too; although, his frequent nightmares had revealed strange memories that weren't his own. While he couldn't fully recollect his predecessor's memories, he had seen more than he should have at Master Maverick's shop.

Manipulation, the gift of using an ancient god's power, was a clearer fit, as he had on multiple occasions called upon Morpheus's power to manifest black flames.

Finally, there was *Interpretation*, the gift of speaking to or understanding the language of the ancient gods, which was undeniable because he frequently conversed with Eteria, Aerus, and Ignis.

"What about the prophetic items?" he mentioned aloud in a rhetorical fashion.

Since the history book on the Reincarnates bore no more fruit, he flipped through the other pages in Master Felix's notebook. Written in bold letters were the prophetic locations that matched items that he had discovered: In Korakk, he had obtained Ignis; In The Talis Mountains, The Tree of Life was supposedly housing another item; In

Avrith, he had still yet to find the bearer of memories; Finally, the location of the heart that hath been lost was still unknown.

"Why is this happening!" he whined, rubbing his temples. "I want to live a normal life. How can I save Gaia?"

"Don't worry, Lucian!" Seraphina exclaimed, trying too hard to sound peppy.

Lucian shot her a disdainful glare and asked, "What do you mean, 'don't worry'? Are you kidding me?"

"Because we're here for you," she stated, confidently.

"Where have I heard that line before?" he sarcastically responded.

He went back to his thoughts, ignoring Seraphina. Idly flipping through the notebook, faint text started to form on one of the pages. Smoothing his finger over the parchment, four items revealed themselves. The fire sword, Ignis, was etched on the top left, a blood-red gem was on the top right, a vial with golden liquid was on the bottom left, and a masked, cloaked figure was on the bottom right. He stared at the parchment, but something felt amiss.

Lucian rummaged in his pockets, pulling out the dirty rock that Master Thaddeus snuck into his pocket along with the letter. He examined it closely, but nothing seemed out of the ordinary. It looked like an average rock.

This can't be it.

While caught up in his own head, Lucian hadn't even noticed that Seraphina had wandered off somewhere.

"Gah!" the girl screamed. "Lucian, help me!"

The heavy padding of feet made him shoot straight up. His head whipped around, trying to figure out the sound's location. A hand gripped his shoulder. He flinched, and the rock in his hand dropped to the floor.

An ensuing *crack!* ascertained the fall, as the rock broke into pieces.

Another set of padding feet echoed throughout the library, coming toward them. Seraphina was shaking behind him, scared of whatever or whoever was approaching them.

He heard a clamor-like sound come from the next row over and then a crash of books.

They both stifled their breaths.

The entity rounded the corner.

Lucian locked eyes with the unidentified creature.

He burst into laughter, while Seraphina fell to her knees in relief and embarrassment.

Lucian approached the tiny creature, extending out his hand to pet the fluffy thing. He recognized the creature from his time in Orsus.

"What is that thing?" she asked, warily.

"It's a Titi," he stated, caressing the tiny creature's head with the palm of his hand. "Just a Titi."

"I'm not just your average Titi," a voice said, proudly. "I'm the Queen of the Titis."

"Hey, Lucian," Seraphina said, her voice shaking like a leaf, "whatever you just did, that's not funny."

Lucian turned his head to look at her while saying, "Wait, I thought you made it talk?"

They both turned their heads back to the Titi, who was still enjoying the petting. Without a doubt in their mind, no matter how absurd, the voice came from the creature.

"What's your problem?" The Titi laughed. "Cat got your tongue?"

4
THE ACADEMY (PART 2)

The Queen of the Titis bowed. Her fluffy frame had collected dust from the bookshelves, so her fur was scruffier than usual. *Swish, swish, swish* went her dark-brown tail, signaling a welcoming gesture.

The Titi deemed a proper introduction necessary, so she stated, "I am Titania, Queen of the Titis. I have traveled from Orsus to see you, young Regulus. I have come to form a Familiar contract with you."

"How very noble of you," he mocked, bowing with exaggerated gestures.

Seraphina flicked the back of his head while saying, "Mind your manners. She's a Queen!"

"Hmm." Lucian squinted his eyes, leaning closer to

analyze the ball of fluff. "Now that you mention it...she *is* a Queen. The Queen of the Furballs."

Seraphina smacked his back so hard that he felt the outline of a handprint searing into his skin. "Hey, what was that for!"

"Mind your manners," she scolded.

"Let me guess," he dryly said, "since you can speak, you must be special."

Titania's tail fluff ruffled in response. "How perceptive of you. Actually, I am—"

He cut her off by saying, "You're a goddess, I presume. A pitiful goddess trapped in a cursed body. Honestly, you gods and goddesses must take me for an utter fool. Let me guess, you're the goddess of mangy mutts."

Titania, clearing her throat, said, "You sure have become more insolent since the last time I saw you. While this title holds no meaning to you, The Regulus's presence is essential for the salvation of humanity. And no, young man, I am not the goddess of mangy mutts. I am the goddess of war."

"So, you *are* the Titi that I saw at Master Maverick's place. No wonder you speak of grandiose and incoherent things," he mused. "You speak of humanity's freedom, but the only freedom you seek is freedom for yourself if I'm not mistaken? Go on. What else have you been hiding from me, Your Majesty?"

Her pointed ears twitched. "Truly, I desire my own freedom but not at the cost of Gaia's life. You of all people should know what's at stake," she said, in a solemn tone. "We gods and goddesses aren't the only ones who are suffering. Humans and gods alike share this burden. Your friend, Aaron, is no different."

A deadly fire ignited in Lucian's veins, coursing through his body and causing his temper to rise. His eyes burned with fury as he warned, "Never say that traitor's name again."

"Calm down!" Seraphina urgently begged, her fingers tugging his cloak. "Please, Lucian..."

Unknowingly, his fists had clenched, fire igniting from his fingertips. The flames burned menacingly, a deep red glow exuding from them. He slowly released the tension in his fist, and the fire extinguished itself. Even the mighty Queen Titania had retreated a couple of feet. Her eyes reflected fear.

"First, let me explain our contract," she said, steadying her breath, "and then I'll give you what you want."

"I'm all ears."

"Much obliged," she said while starting her explanation. "First, our contract is in effect until one of us dies or when you, the contractor, decides to end it. Second, I draw my power from your mana, so anything that happens to me happens to you. Third, your commands are a law to me as long as the contract symbol on your hand remains."

"You said that you would give me what I want?" he asked, lessening the sharpness in his tone.

"I promise to alleviate the symptoms of the curse and the restrictive spell cast on your companions that blocked your communication with them."

So that's why Aerus and Ignis wouldn't speak to me. He lamented. *Why didn't I notice it sooner?*

"I have one more condition," Lucian stated.

"I will comply with any condition that is within my control," she affirmed.

"You must never lie to me." He stared seriously into her amber eyes. "If you lie to me, then the contract will be forfeited."

"Do you not trust me?"

"Hah." He scoffed. "I only trust those who tell me the truth—the whole truth. Do we have a deal, Queen Titania?"

"You're aware of the ancient customs," Titania stated. "A Familiar's contract works the same way. Just reenact what you've learned."

He needed something sharp.

He needed something that could break his skin.

Instead of staining Ignis with his blood, Lucian reached into his cloak, retrieving Master Felix's long-forgotten scepter. Examining the purple gem on top, he ascertained its properties. No incantation was cast; instead, he quickly slit the flesh of his index finger with the gem's pointy edge. It was easier than finding a knife.

A look of recognition appeared to cross Titania's scruffy face. Her enveloping black eyes narrowed as she focused on the scepter.

"Where did you get that scepter?" Titania suspiciously asked. "And that gem..."

"You can ask Master Felix the next time you see him," Lucian sarcastically said.

He reached down, allowing the Titi to lick the blood with her smooth tongue, sealing the contract. He felt something burning on the backside of his right hand. He looked down at his hand, noticing a strange symbol etched into his skin.

He noted the symbol etched into his skin. The symbol comprised of two red swords crossing each other and a black bird's wings wrapped around their hilts. It pulsated and then slowly faded away.

"Is that all?" Lucian asked.

"Not all, but it's good enough, for now," she stated with a relieved tone. "I will fulfill my end of the bargain."

Lucian momentarily looked around, noticing that Seraphina had once again disappeared. He flushed any minimal concern for her well-being out of his mind.

Good riddance. No more nagging.

Titania mumbled, as her eyes were sealed shut. She slowly stepped closer toward him. An ethereal, white light emitted from her petite body.

He gulped down any semblance of fear swirling within him. Standing still, he watched as the Titi spoke her stream of incantations. She was close enough to bite his face. Her tiny, wet nose tapped his chest, the area where the blue dot was.

A white light sprang off the Titi onto him like a fish jumping out of water. It passed through his clothes, seeping into his body's cursed regions.

A warm yet purifying sensation streamed through the blue tendrils, transforming the dark, icky blue into a pure white color, reverting the skin to its original pigment. Once the white had completely devoured the blue, the heavy, almost suffocating symptoms of the curse vanished. Almost instantly, his wicked mood dissipated.

"What did you do?" he asked, sincerely, the weight in his heart lightening by the second.

"Curses are cruel and taint even the purest of souls. Even you are no exception to their effects," Titania explained, smiling warmly. "While I couldn't fully cure the curse, you shouldn't suffer from the side effects anymore."

He felt ashamed of his actions, but he was equally confused by the situation. "You couldn't cure the curse...?"

A sudden rattling at his hip distracted him. Ignis shook in his sheath, reacting violently out of nowhere. Even when Lucian tried to settle the sword down, the shaking intensified. He winced at the heat generated by the sword.

Come on, Ignis. Calm down!

"What an impatient vessel," Titania mumbled, pressing her nose to the sword's burning blade. Her wet nose seemed to lessen the sting of the heat, but the contact of the nose to metal still smelled like burning flesh to him.

"*Exsolvo!*" she chanted.

The restrictive magic spell on the sword disappeared, a burst of inappropriate words pouring out from Ignis's consciousness.

"You ungrateful mongrel of a brat! How dare you confine the mighty Ignis to a measly auditory restraining spell! I'll burn you alive like the swine you are, Aaron!" the sword sang out in a disharmonious tone. "If I see that mutt ever again, I'll roast him alive!"

"Don't worry, Ignis. You won't need to roast him alive, because I'll drive your blade straight through his heart."

"Phew!" Ignis exclaimed. "What a little warrior you've become. Looks like a good betrayal or two can be very effective!"

"Don't mock him!" Titania scolded. "This never would've happened if you had properly protected him in the first place!"

"Blah, blah, blah," the sword mocked. "You have no right to doubt me, for I am his most trustworthy companion!"

"Just because you're Morpheus's sword, it doesn't mean all of your actions are excusable!" she shouted.

Lucian's mind spun as he asked, "Morpheus...you mean...you're his sword? I should've left you in that serpent's stomach. Ha! You knew all along, and yet you..."

"Titania, you little—" Ignis cursed, releasing a wave of red haze.

"Enough!" Lucian commanded. "What else have you been hiding from me? Let me guess, there's something else, isn't there?"

A swell of emotions enveloped him.

"Calm down," Ignis said. "It's not like Eteria, Aerus, and I didn't want to tell you the truth. We simply didn't know whether you were ready for it or not."

"So, all of you were in cahoots." Lucian snorted, darkness creeping back into his heart. "Tell me the truth this instant, or I swear I'll send you into the depths of The Fallen Realm myself."

"No," Ignis refused. "We are at fault for deceiving you, but the whole truth... Well, it's something that you'll have to see with your own eyes. Our lips are sealed. Quite literally sealed, since we, the Fallen gods, are under the curse of..."

"The curse of...?" Lucian repeated.

"We can't reveal the name of the one who cursed us," the sword admitted.

"Fine," Lucian stated, harshly. "Then, tell me something you *can* say."

Ignis seemed to hesitate, but a certain resolve bled through his silence. He finally spoke. "Lucian, you're undeniably the Reincarnate of the Fallen god, Morpheus. As such, your very soul is tied to his own. His memories, regrets, and powers are within you, festering to break free. Your nightmares hold more meaning than you think."

"Stop speaking in vague terms," Lucian demanded. "I've had enough of your riddles. I want the truth."

"Okay, okay, okay, be patient," the sword stated. "What I'm saying is, your nightmares aren't *just* nightmares. Everything that you see while asleep or unconscious is connected to Morpheus's memories or is prophesying some future event."

"All of them...?" Lucian asked, the tension in his body spiking. "You mean, Adonis's betrayal...Caelum's destruction...Rosalie's death...all of those are...real?"

Lucian broke into a fit of maniacal laughter. He sank to the floor, despair crashing over him like waves mercilessly hitting the sand. His fingers pulled at his mess of blond strands. His internal pain matched his external breakdown.

Is this my future? Am I truly the killer of my flesh, the destroyer of my home, and the curse of this world?

As if to distract Lucian from his mental deterioration, Ignis went off on some tangent and started to ramble. "You would think the other two would've already intervened in our conversation. Haha. I mean, Aerus has never been much of a talker, but Eteria... Where is that annoying goddess when you need her anyway? At such an important time!"

A momentary release from his breakdown, Lucian stated with a deep-seated resentment, "Aaron took her... When he cast me down into my death, he broke the cord and stole her."

"Ah, ha, ha, ha!" Ignis let out a burst of fake laughter. "I guess she finally got what she deserved!"

"If you so much as say another word, then I'll drive your blade into acid and let you melt into a pile of miserable slag."

Silence ensued, until...

"Lucian, look what I found!" Seraphina exclaimed, barreling through the halls with a bounce in her step. Held above her head was a thin royal-blue book with a stretch of numbers etched across its cover. She seemed to completely disregard the heavy mood. She thrust the book at him, leaving him puzzled but not in the mood to ask questions.

Lucian flipped through the pages, realizing it was some

sort of record book. Each section had its own special unit name with a dozen headshots of students. They wore matching uniforms of black robes with colored ties or bows.

Amongst the hundreds of unrecognized faces, his eyes rested on two names: Ferris Rode and Leon Alastair. Leon looked the same, as his hair was white, and his face was youthful. However, the picture above the nameplate "Ferris Rode" was not recognizable.

Instead of the pale, ginger-haired man that he had been mentored by, a stranger had replaced him: a pudgy male student with oily, dirty-blonde hair and dark-brown eyes.

Even as Lucian's mental state was in tatters, the disconnect between the unfamiliar face and the familiar name couldn't be overlooked. His heart, which burned with anger, froze into ice. He stared down at the sword, into Titania's eyes, and then back at the book.

"Who is he?"

No response.

"Don't make me repeat myself," he threatened.

"Lucian, please, don't fall back into darkness," Titania pleaded. "Look, you're scaring Seraphina."

Evil chattered in his ears, clouding his consciousness. His vision narrowed. He could only see straight in front of him—nothing else. "Tell. Me. The. Truth." His voice deepened.

"Ferris Rode is..." Titania started, her entire body shaking. Her eyes flitted back and forth nervously.

"Come on," he stated. "Just tell me."

Her ears and tail drooped.

"Tell me."

With the pads of her paws, she swiped at the record book's pages, turning them until she reached the desired one. Her right paw rested on the name of his mentor, Felix Knight, whose smiling face was etched into the parchment.

His hands shook uncontrollably. The full name of his beloved mentor echoed in his head like an endless curse...

"Ferris Rode," she revealed, "is actually Felix Knight."

5
THE REGULUS

 *Bluewater*

The chill of dawn evoked a silent sorrow. Streams of salty sweat drizzled down his pale face. With his brows knit tightly together, he fervently swung the stubborn sword. The nauseating stench of sweat and copper assaulted him. The callouses on his palms burst, staining Ignis's intricate, embroidered hilt with thick, bloody smudges.

His arm muscles screamed.

His legs wobbled beneath him.

His nightmares resurfaced.

"Who could ever love a Fallen One?"

The cold sun rose steadily, higher and higher into the cloudless, blue sky. An eerie silence surrounded him: No birds chirped, and no trees rustled. Like mice's soft chatter, he heard low yet audible voices escape the cracks of The Broken Latch's back door.

"Shouldn't we say something?" a girl's voice whispered, urgency heightening her tone. "He hasn't eaten, slept, or washed for two days. I've left food for him on the back doorstep, but he refuses to eat. Oh, Master Leon, please, I beg you, do something! He'll starve at this rate!"

"Well, I'll see what I can do," Leon said, calmly. "I can't possibly shove the food down his throat, now, can I?"

"Hmph! I never asked you to!"

A set of footsteps stomped away.

Lucian breathed out a sigh, continuing his repetitious swinging motion. *I won't die from two days without food*, he internally countered, remembering his childhood suffering. *This is nothing compared to those days... Seraphina should really...*

"Mind her own business, right?" Leon's voice broke through the silence. He suddenly appeared and casually leaned on the doorframe with a food tray. "I keep telling her that you won't drop dead, but she doesn't believe me. I know that you're processing everything right now, but at least try to eat to appease her. She's genuinely worried about you."

"Worried about me?" He scoffed. "If she was really worried about me, then she should've just left me for dead by the river. At least then I would've been free from this burden."

"A burden it may be, child," the man stated, "but it's a burden you must bear. Whether by fate or by curse, you are The Regulus."

"Regulus this, Regulus that!" Lucian sliced the air, sweat leaping off him. "I'm only sixteen years old! What are you people expecting from me? I'm not a pawn!"

"We never said you were a pawn," Leon denied. "You're our only hope. The gods and goddesses have chosen you. No, that's not quite correct. Felix chose you. He trusted you to save The Earthly Realm and The Fallen Ones. Are you going to betray his trust?"

How am I supposed to save The Earthly Realm and The Fallen Ones, if I can't even manage to save myself? Lucian internally questioned. *I'm tired of being lied to. I'm tired of not knowing who I can trust. I'm tired of the gods intervening in my life.*

"I can't promise you peace, but I can promise you my protection, loyalty, and power," Leon stated. "I won't ask that you trust me. I only ask that you fulfill your destiny as The Regulus."

"How can I accept your loyalty, if you won't even reveal your true identity?" Lucian argued. "Sense revealed to me that you aren't a normal human, but you also aren't a Reincarnate. Who, no, what, are you?"

"I'm a specter of the past," the man responded, solemnly. "I'm nothing more than a pebble on your path. I'll tell you my identity, but it won't change what must be done... I am Leon, the god of restoration."

"Leon?" Lucian questioned, faintly remembering who the god was. His mind flashed back to his former lessons about the ancient gods.

"Ah, that Leon... Does Seraphina know?"

"No, she doesn't, and I ask that you don't tell her. It's something that I need to say, personally. Now's not the time...not yet." Lucian saw a weary smile appear on the man's face. "Our little chat is over. I'm sure that you're famished. Eat before the food gets cold again."

"Wait." Lucian reached out his hand. "There's something that I still don't understand. Why are you in human form, when your Fallen comrades are bound to objects like swords and beasts like serpents?"

"We were tethered to the things we love most," the man replied, "and cursed by them much the same."

With those cryptic words, Leon went inside the shop, leaving Lucian alone with his thoughts.

Lucian's iron grip on Ignis's hilt loosened, and the sword hit the dewy grass. He opened and closed his palms, assessing the damage. His muscles screeched in pain as he walked toward the meal. He plopped onto the backdoor step, devouring the warm beef and slurping down the cool water.

"Hah!" Lucian exclaimed, his belly feeling satisfied.

"Hey, Lucian!" Ignis called out from the grass. "Please don't ignore me! It's been two whole days since you've even cursed at me! You haven't said anything, and now, a filthy bug's climbing up my blade! Hey! Help me!"

"What do you mean, I haven't been talking to you?" Lucian asked, bewildered. "I was just talking to—"

The dots connected like clockwork.

A chill ran down his spine.

He broke into a cold sweat, thinking, *Could Leon have been reading my mind this entire time? I think I'm going to throw up...*

His mind swirled.

His stomach gurgled.

He threw up.

After emptying out his entire stomach, Lucian lay on his back, staring at the sky. His throat and chest burned, while his eyes wearily drooped. Fatigue slowly crept up his body like a spider to a web. He held up his hand, outlining the scratches and stains.

Closing his fingers into a fist, he muttered to himself, "Why me...?"

He fell into a daze.

"Lucian!" a sweet voice called. "It's time to wake up!"

Lucian roused himself out of a hazy state. His eyes were still adjusting to the sunlight, and the figure approaching him was blurry. Walking toward him was a petite, young lady with a gentle aura. She reminded him of his sister.

"Rosalie." He coughed. "Is that you...?"

"No, silly!" She laughed, a comforting smile painting her lips. "It's me, Seraphina!"

Snapping back into reality, the rosy filter around the girl died as a flame extinguished. He stretched out his sore muscles, each crack reminding him of his previous activities. The nostalgic warmth of his sister vanished with disappointment in its place. He stood up.

"What are you doing?" Lucian let out a low snarl. He flicked off the blades of grass clinging to his cloak. "Did Leon send you?"

"Ever the suspicious one, aren't you?" Seraphina retorted. "I was just making sure that you weren't dead. I wouldn't want our backyard to reek of a rotting corpse and scare away any of our customers. If you're going to die, then die somewhere else."

"Witch," he mumbled.

"I. HEARD. THAT." She playfully kicked him.

"Alright, alright, I'm sorry!" he forfeited. "What do you want?"

"Master Leon needs to speak with you," she said,

pointing to the store. "He's at his worktable. Oh, yeah! He also said that you need to bring Ignis with you."

Lucian shot Ignis a sharp glare.

"We already spoke earlier..." he muttered, hopelessly.

"Lucian, we're your friends. We're just trying to help you." She grinned, lightly smacking his back.

"Friends?" he asked, genuinely shocked. "I'm not exactly looking for any friends..."

"You're so dramatic," she stated, rolling her eyes. "Everyone needs a friend or two."

"Well, you know how great it went the last time I made a friend."

"Lucian, just think about that time as a season."

"Why a season?"

"Because it'll pass," she replied. "One day, the pain of your past will be overshadowed by the joy of your present."

"When will that time arrive?"

"Soon. Until then, just learn to love yourself for who you are and don't worry what other people think about you."

"It seems like you're talking about yourself."

She blushed slightly and said, "Well, all good advice comes from personal experience."

"How's your advice working out for you?"

"It's...a work in progress." She chuckled. "You're the

first step in the right direction. You're the first person I've wanted to become friends with, after all."

"Why me...?" he asked, hesitantly.

Seraphina stared at the sky and said, "Because you treat me like a person, not a monster. My red hair is considered a curse here." Her fists clenched.

"Well, I know a lot about curses." He unexpectedly played along, a light smile flashing on his face. "I can't promise anything, but I'll consider your offer."

"You finally smiled!" she happily exclaimed.

"Huh?" He looked confused. "Did I?"

"You know what Master Leon always says?" she rhetorically asked.

"A sword can break anyone's smile?" he jested.

"No, no." She shook her head and wagged her index finger at him. "Just as a sword can take a life, a simple smile can, in turn, save one."

He stood mesmerized by her wisdom.

"Now that we've had a good talk." She clapped her hands together. "It's time for you to see Master Leon."

THE ATMOSPHERE WAS UNCOMFORTABLY QUIET—awkward, even. Lucian watched as Leon meticulously worked on a broken, metal lock. Not a word was exchanged between them.

In Leon's right hand was a tiny, metal tool with a twisted top. He kept tinkering, turning the tool in the lock while taking out a few steel pins. Once the cover of the lock was removed, he was able to focus on the internal cylinder and locking mechanism. A bead of sweat trickled down his forehead. The concentration level for such a detailed job seemed far too taxing for what the repair's cost was worth.

"Ahem." Lucian coughed. "Seraphina, um, said you needed to speak with me."

"Ah, yes." Leon continued fiddling with the lock, not even meeting Lucian's gaze. "I took a look at some of your items when you were unconscious, but I wanted to wait until you were awake to do a detailed inspection."

"Why?"

"I thought you wanted transparency."

"I do," he admitted. "I just am a bit confused lately... about everything."

"Don't worry, kid," Leon said, reassuringly. "You're not the only one in a tight spot."

Emptying his pockets, Lucian placed Ignis, Master Felix's scepter and notebook, Aaron's note, and Eva's ring on the worktable.

A soft twinkle shimmered in the locksmith's eyes. They seemed to flit back and forth between Master Felix's scepter and Ignis.

He's acting like a child who got a new toy.

The locksmith smoothed back his unruly, white hair. Something about the scepter and the sword fascinated him.

"Who gave you this scepter?"

Leon turned the scepter in his hands, searching for an inscription.

"Let me just tell you that the answer to most of your questions will be Master Felix," Lucian said, sardonically.

Leon held the scepter up to the light, analyzing the purple gemstone embedded in it.

"Did he tell you what this purple gem is?"

Lucian shook his head.

"It's an El Stone," the man revealed. "Not only that, but it's also a very special El Stone."

"Why so?"

"Before I explain, are you aware of what an El Stone is?"

"Yes, Barren explained the basics back at Korakk," Lucian stated.

"Did he teach you about each of their unique attributes?"

"No." Lucian shook his head. "Barren only told me that they stored mana, healed minor injuries, and the like."

"Each El Stone has special magical attributes. Think of The El Stones as an energy source and a power amplifier. Any Mage would pay a pretty credit for one," Leon explained. "And you have *Storm*, one of the most powerful El Stones."

"Aren't Storm's attributes *lightning* and *water*?" he questioned. "They have the same magical attributes as Aaron's abilities, so won't they clash?"

"No, child, Storm's attributes are *Darkness* and *Fire*." The locksmith flashed him a wide and confident smile. "These attributes match perfectly with your magical affinities. Ah, I knew Felix was a genius, but I didn't know that he'd be this forward-thinking!"

"Why is it called *Storm*, then?"

"Uh, well," he chuckled, diverting the conversation. "It's still an appropriate name for this El Stone. When paired with a Mage that has one or both affinities, The El Stone will produce a royal-purple flame that moves as fast as lightning."

"So, why is Storm the best for fighting Aaron?"

"Aaron's Lightning attribute increases the base speed of his attacks, which allows him to overwhelm his opponents; however, Storm's effects can easily match that speed," he explained. "Additionally, Storm's abilities, when combined with Ignis's flames, will greatly increase the intensity of his flames."

"I am not a mere tool that you can enhance!" Ignis sneered. "I am perfect as-is."

"Such ego," Leon conceded.

Without warning, Leon took Ignis in his grasp. Swiftly and aptly, he infused his mana into the very bottom of the sword's blade, creating a tiny gem-shaped hole. Ignis cried in feigned pain. Leon proceeded to wedge The El Stone, Storm, into the forged hole.

"I'll roast you alive until you're nothing more than ashes one of these days, Leon," Ignis threatened. "Even if you are one of us."

Lucian completely tuned out the conversation. All of this El Stone talk reminded him of Aaron. His mind returned to the revelation of Aaron's Dragonian Curse and the time when he wanted to alleviate his former friend's pain. The memory in the bar with Barren resurfaced, forcing Lucian to remember how he had stupidly empathized with Aaron's sob story. If he had known The El Stone was in his possession, would he have foolishly gifted it to the one person who would later betray him? Would he still have rushed to save him?

"No," Lucian mumbled to himself, sadly but surely. He steeled himself, a slow-burning flame rising within him. "If it's a fight he wants, then it's a fight he'll get."

6

SEA OF STARS

 *Bluewater*

A sea of stars stretched into infinity. Lucian approached a broad figure—a figure idly staring into the night sky.

Rubbing the weariness from his eyes, he asked, "Leon, it's almost midnight. What's so important that it couldn't wait until the morning?"

"The truth," Leon said, solemnly. His hands reached out to the stars and to The Heavenly Realm. "Ah, what a beautiful night you've brought us, Astro."

Sitting down next to the wistful man, Lucian mumbled to himself, "I've never heard of a god paying respects to another god before."

"In the morning, Titania will return to guide you to

The Tree of Life." The man ignored his comment and pointed in the direction of The Talis Mountains. "She's been scouting the area the entire day in preparation of your next mission."

Lucian's brows furrowed. He hadn't fully accepted his duty as The Regulus, but he couldn't just sit around and do nothing while Aaron ran amok.

"Are you really going to tell me the truth?" Lucian asked, skeptically.

"I swear on the stars in the sky that I will tell you the truth," Leon promised. "Just as the stars reveal to us their secrets each night, so shall I."

"Can I ask you anything I want, then?"

"If it's within my knowledge and my ability to, then I will." Leon reassuringly patted Lucian's shoulder. "Let me remind you that I too am under a curse, so I can't reveal our enemy's identity."

"I understand." Lucian nodded.

"Since Titania will take you to The Talis Mountains in the morning, the daybreak is your time limit. Ask your first question whenever you're ready."

A wave of uncertainty washed over Lucian. He had so many questions, so much time to ask them... But somewhere deep inside of him, he shivered with fear... Fear of the unknown. Fear of the truth—his much-desired truth.

He gulped down his hesitation and then asked, "So, let

me get this straight... Ferris Rode is Master Felix... But who is *he*, truly?"

"Ah, I knew you'd ask me this question." Leon chuckled, looking at the moon. "Felix is, well, an anomaly, isn't he? Ferris Rode is his public alias whenever he travels. His acting is convincing, isn't it? However, his true name is Felix Knight, the official Magus of Lunaris and the strongest Mage within Eva's organization."

"Why does Aaron share the same last name as him, then?" he questioned, with a faltering tone. "I thought Rena and Barren raised him."

"You're right," Leon admitted. "They oversaw his training and teaching. Even so, Felix thought it best to have Aaron take his last name, seeing as the surnames 'Croft' and 'Xanthus' come with troubling affiliations. Best to let the two of them explain their family histories to you later."

All of the incoming information settled in his brain, replacing the lies he had been told by Aaron with the experiences he shared with the other alliance members.

"Felix was sent to Caelum to find the prophetic child. He was sent to find you," Leon explained. "He even brought support, but things didn't turn out as he had expected. We thought it would be a quick trip, but Caelum is hard to enter for any outsider, let alone a powerful Mage like Felix. We had to make some sacrifices, change some plans, and firmly ground ourselves in the village before we could convince the overly suspicious Elders. What we needed most was their trust, and that very trust took over a decade to acquire."

The Elders. Lucian scowled at the sound of their mention. *Those filthy monsters...*

A strange feeling rose in his chest, as Lucian asked, "What happened to Master Felix's support?"

"I can't say for sure," Leon answered. "The details of this mission were as confidential as could be. Whether man or woman, I couldn't say. All I know is that he or she would've had constant contact with Felix in some way or another and been able to relay information about you to him regularly."

Lucian couldn't believe the amount of effort his mentor put in to lay the groundwork for his future. Lost to his astonishment, the identity of Master Felix's support lingered in his mind as even more questions arose.

Lucian's questions spread to even more mysteries. Something deep within him pressed him to ask further.

"You keep talking about your organization, but what exactly is it?" Lucian asked, eager for more answers. "I know Eva was the founder, but who are the other members?"

"Our organization's name is the 'Alliance of The Fallen' or 'ATF' for short. And I must apologize in advance. I only know of the members on my route. We have several main traveling routes with informants based in each nation... Felix of Caelum, Maverick of Lunaris, Barren of Korakk, Rena of Faeran, and our leader, Evangeline of Terras."

"Woah." Lucian's eyes lit up with excitement. "Wait, does that mean there are even more?"

"Yes, many." Leon nodded, his glossy, silver hair shimmering in the moonlight. "I'm only aware of the stationed informants. Traveling informants are under a different division."

"How did you know, though?" Lucian asked, his forehead wrinkling with confusion. "How did you know that I was Morpheus's Reincarnate? Did Master Felix tell you?"

"No, but all I needed to do was wait for Eva's prophecy to fulfill itself," Leon stated. "I trust her, so I knew you or whoever The Regulus was would arrive sometime soon. Her prophecies tend to come true, after all."

Lucian pulled some grass sprouting beneath him, prepping for his next question.

"Then, you must know about what I've done and what I'll do in the future..." Lucian stated, biting his lip. "Is what Ignis said true? Will my nightmares become my future reality? Will I destroy Caelum? Will I kill them... kill her?

"Dreams aren't always what they appear to be, Lucian," Leon explained. "I don't know what you saw in your dreams, but prophecies aren't always set in stone. Although we seek prophecies for guidance, the circumstances can change. I'm not sure what else to tell you."

"Am I truly the monster everyone feared me to be?" Lucian crumpled his hair in his hands. "Will I become my family's curse again?"

"You aren't a curse," Leon assured, patting him on the back. "The fact that you fear that outcome means you possess a caring heart. If you hold onto who you are, you won't fall into the enemy's trap or let the curse consume you. Our organization wants you to save Gaia, but the only one who can truly save you is yourself."

"About my curse..." Lucian asked, looking down at the lingering blue spot on his body. "What is it? Why can't it be cured?"

"That's..." Leon started to say, but his words trailed off.

Seeing that he wouldn't receive an answer, Lucian pushed through to another question.

"Why does this mysterious god want to destroy Gaia?" He peered far off into the stretch of hills, the grass rising and falling like the waves of The Portacle Sea. "What does he gain by controlling my body and killing everyone?"

"Revenge, I suppose," Leon revealed, spitting the words out like poison. "I was never close to Morpheus or Adonis myself, but I do know that before The Heavenly Pillars fell, they had a harrowing encounter with *him*."

"What do my nightmares mean, then?" Lucian asked, impatiently. "Morpheus's memories reside within me, but they're contradictory and confusing. In one of my dreams, I witnessed Morpheus and Adonis fighting each other at The Heavenly Pillars."

"You should ask Felix about Morpheus," Leon stated. "He knows more about the ancient god of destruction than anyone else..."

If I ever see him again...

Moving onto his next question, Lucian asked, "The Fallen Ones... I thought they were just the residents of The Fallen District in Caelum, but they're something else, right?"

"The Fallen Ones are the gods and goddesses who have been cursed by the enemy. While some of us were spared from imprisonment in The Fallen Realm, most of my brethren have been sealed. Unable to ascend to The Earthly Realm, their souls remain trapped in an endless stasis."

The Fallen Realm? I thought that place was just a myth...

Switching to a lighter subject, Leon interrupted his thoughts by saying, "Before you ask any more questions, you need to know the meaning behind your mission."

"My travels seem like a wild goose chase," Lucian said, sarcasm rolling off his tongue.

"Eva prophesied that you, the reincarnation of

Morpheus, would become The Regulus, the savior of Gaia. However, for you to become The Regulus of the prophecy, you need to unlock the full potential and powers of Morpheus himself. Not only were you assigned from birth to unlock the four gifts of the Reincarnates: Sense, Connection, Manipulation, and Interpretation, but you were also tasked to retrieve Morpheus's scattered possessions. One of which was his sword, Ignis."

"So, I've been collecting his possessions this entire time..." Lucian lay back on the grass, drawing out a long sigh.

While they conversed back and forth, the sun started to peek out of the nightly abyss. "I have another question," Lucian said, trying to extend the time limit. "Can you tell me more about The Tree of Life, and what I'm supposed to retrieve from it? This specific mission honestly sounds like a death sentence, seeing as it's in the dragon's territory."

"Oh, you won't have to worry about those flies." Leon chuckled. "If anything, you'll have to worry more about... Well, there's no use in scaring you, now. According to the written records about Morpheus, you have to retrieve a vial of The Tree of Life's sap. The sap is said to have incredible healing properties, which can completely revive someone on the brink of death... But there's a price. Whoever dares steal sap from The Tree of Life must risk his life to save another."

Sending me to my death, I see, Lucian scoffed.

"Is Seraphina perchance a Reincarnate?" Lucian asked, out of the blue. "Or a Fallen goddess who's lost her memories?"

"She's the last person to lose her memories," Leon chuckled. "As for your question, you'll have to wait and find out for yourself."

Since the sun was in the sky, Leon rose to leave. However, Lucian begged to ask one last question. Images of Eva's death flashed in Lucian's mind, especially Aaron's reaction. It was unusual that he didn't seem to care about Eva's death. Although Aaron was a callous traitor, Lucian had some hope left for his humanity.

"You keep talking about Eva as if she's still living in the present." Lucian braced for the answer. "I saw Eva's corpse back in Lunaris... Do you know what happened to her?"

"Ah," Leon recalled. "The Soulless must've confronted her. I suppose it's alright if I tell you the truth, now."

"Tell me...what?"

"Eva's not dead," Leon revealed, a half-smile spreading across his face. "We spoke the other day."

"What did she say?"

"She wanted me to ask you something." Leon's expression turned serious.

"Ask me...what?"

"If Aaron had tried to kill you before."

An unwanted memory resurfaced: the gleam of the knife and the curses of his companion. Lucian nodded.

"Ah, then it has already begun." Leon swept several silver hair strands from his face.

"What? What's already begun?" Lucian's brain refused to cooperate. Flashes of the mana-devouring tendrils popped into his mind. "His countdown to death?"

"No." Leon shook his head. "He's not dying, at all..."

"Then, what is it!?" Lucian's tone spiked. "If not death, then what?"

"He's turning into a *Soulless*."

7

TO SAVE A
SOUL (PART I)

S oulless. Soulless. Soulless. That nasty word kept creeping into Lucian's head like a snake—a snake that was currently slithering its way down into the pit of his stomach. Aaron was becoming a creature worse than death. He was becoming one of the Soulless.

The images of the Soulless—those creatures that wrapped themselves in shadows and malice with pale-white bodies and grotesquely long limbs hung in his mind, causing his entire body to shutter. He felt his own life being sucked out of him just thinking about them.

"Lucian, are you even listening to me?" Titania threatened, her voice breaking through his inner turmoil.

"Ah, yes," he replied with a dazed tone. "You were lecturing me about the history of The Tree of Life, right?"

"Yeah, about five minutes ago, Lucian," she stated, letting out a long, exasperated sigh. "You know, you really should be taking this mission more seriously."

Seraphina came to his defense by exclaiming, "He is taking it seriously! He just needs some time to adjust, that's all. Right, Lucian?"

He nodded his head, as his eyes drooped from a night's lack of sleep. He let out a yawn to the annoyance of the aggravated Titi walking ahead of him. Titania sighed once more, as she explained, "No one has been near The Tree of Life in many centuries. As you've learned from the bordering villages, none of their villagers will even step foot at its base. I've heard a lot of rumors about The Tree of Life... Let's just say that we should stay on alert."

"What do you mean?" Lucian inquired.

"Hmm, I've heard those rumors too," Seraphina said, her voice trailing in from behind him. "Even though they've been extinct for centuries, everyone in Avrith believes a dragon is guarding the tree. People in Faeran believe that it's an evil fairy, though."

A trickle of sweat ran down Lucian's forehead. "Why are we doing this again?" he asked, almost sheepishly. "I don't want to die...not again."

"You are The Regulus, child," Titania stated. "It's your destiny."

A destiny to die! he internally exclaimed. *I might as well be served on a silver plate and have a label on me that reads, "Dragon Fodder."*

Out of the sheath wrapped around his waist came a burst of laughter. "You never cease to amuse me!" Ignis proclaimed, laughter reverberating through his blade. "Dragon fodder! Ha! You, a boy of only skin and bones?"

Lucian lifted the sword out of the sheath and said with a cold tone, "One more laugh, and I'll throw you off the mountain. Got it?"

Lucian slid Ignis back into his sheath, the laughter immediately ceasing. From behind, Seraphina rested her hand on his shoulder. While she didn't say a word, he understood what her gesture meant. He took a deep breath to lessen the building tension and continued walking on the trail at a hastier pace to catch up with his guide.

Once Lucian reached Titania, the scenery, which had been covered by clouds, changed, turning into something magnificent. The three of them had left at dawn, so by the time that they were traveling up The Talis Mountains, the sky was like a vibrant sea filled with orange flames.

The clouds spread out into infinity, some forming marvelous floating ships and others forming serene waves. Even The Talis Mountains themselves were fantastic. Every time that Lucian visited them, their beauty captivated him. The streaming light from the emerging sun reflected off the purple mountaintops, turning them into glittering gems.

Before he knew it, Seraphina was to his right, marveling at the scenery. The words slipped from his mouth, as he stared toward the sun and said, "How beautiful."

Seraphina's head turned toward him, eyes interlocking with each other.

"The sky," he blurted out, his face flushing a bright red. "I meant the sky is beautiful."

He scratched his head, awkwardly.

She let out a light chuckle. Her lips formed a precious smile, and her eyes crinkled with happiness. She mouthed the words, "I know," and they continued walking in silence.

AFTER A FEW MORE HOURS OF WALKING, THE group finally reached their destination. Lucian looked to the sky, where the sun had almost reached its peak. Strangely enough, their destination wasn't at the apex of The Talis Mountains, but rather it was only halfway up.

"I'm going to throw up," he said, dramatically. He clasped his hand over his mouth, feigning sick. With one eye open, he looked to see if Seraphina or Titania bought his bit.

When they seemed unfazed by his outburst, he whined, "How much longer?"

Seraphina chuckled at his silliness and playfully said, "Maybe a few more hours?"

Lucian lost all hope, exaggeratedly collapsing to the ground. Titania seemed to either not notice his whining or didn't care for his theatrics. Her eyes were locked onto the extremely dark cave sitting ominously before them.

A howling noise rang out from the depths of the cave, reverberating off the stone and rock walls. Cold air rushed straight at his face, sending chills through his core. He watched as the fur on her back shot up. Her wariness sent a wave of fear into him.

Still lying on the ground, Lucian crawled over to the edge of The Talis Mountains.

A tiny thought popped into his mind, *Jumping off the mountain doesn't seem so bad now that I think about it... Anything's better than this hell that I'm being forced to walk into.*

Titania peered back at him, knowing exactly what he was thinking at that moment. He smothered the thought of escaping and resigned himself to his fate. Pushing himself off the rocky ground, he followed his furry friend into the cave. Seraphina trailed behind them.

Time seemed to stand still, as the chilly wind ceased once they entered. A sense of foreboding crawled into him. Just like Titania, his neck hairs shot straight up.

After several minutes of walking in the dark, a circle of light appeared in the near distance. The further they walked, the clearer the opening became.

Salvation! he cried internally, the sight of light lulling him into a false sense of security.

Seraphina grabbed onto his shoulder again, but this time, it was different. Her hand squeezed tighter, refusing to release him. Whatever was ahead of them was bad news. They reached the circle of light, which was just the opening between the dark tunnel and the main area of the cave. They cautiously passed through it. His eyes readjusted for a few seconds. Once Lucian could see again, he was stunned.

A giant, pure-white, ethereal tree sat in the center of a glistening stream of water. There were breaks at the top of the cave, allowing natural sunlight to illuminate the tree. Its petals were like crystals, reflecting off rays of light and brightening the area around them. He couldn't help but want to touch the tree. His body started to walk toward it in a trance-like state. With his arm outstretched, he calmly headed toward the center of the cave.

At some point, he heard Seraphina's voice yelling something, but he couldn't quite decipher her words. They seeped into the shallow waters that his feet were treading through. His consciousness slid into darkness, slowly dragging him deeper into the abyss.

Even when a flash of magic whirled past him, hitting the tree's barrier, he was too spellbound. Too lost. Another blast of magic flew past him, this time destroying the barrier. It broke the illusion. The false image of The Tree of Life with all of its wonders shattered. The sparkling vision created by the barrier left a lifeless, rotting lump of bark in its place.

Seeping out of The Tree of Life was an outpouring of malice, its surface roots stretching out to him like a witch's spindly fingers. He regained control of his mental clarity, finally hearing Seraphina screaming, "It's a trap!"

But it was too late.

Lucian fumbled to unsheathe Ignis, a stroke of luck saving him from a branch striking his throat. The blade clashed against a second branch reaching for him, throwing him backward. He hit the water hard. With Ignis's blade, Lucian blocked another branch attacking from his side.

Retreating as far as he could, he thought he had escaped The Tree of Life's range. He was wrong. His legs were trapped in the waters, thick, green vegetation holding him still. He tried cutting through them, but his efforts were in vain.

Slice after slice, nothing seemed to work. Shooting red flames through the vegetation loosened their hold, but more vegetation replaced the scorched ones. This pattern repeated itself, while the spiky branches lunged at him. Just as quickly as the barrier was broken by Seraphina's spells, it was restored at the same pace.

Lucian quickly looked behind him, seeing Seraphina and Titania trying to break the barrier again. With each attempt, the barrier came back stronger than before. They were struggling. He was struggling. A moment's weakness led to this horror. He felt his strength leaving him. The vegetation sapped his mana.

"Ignis!" he yelled, calling forth brilliant red flames from the blade. "*Combustum!*"

The surface of the water caught fire, spirals of red riding the waves and latching onto the tree's outstretched and attacking branches. The vegetation restraining him, the waters surrounding him, and the roots attacking him burned.

A wave of relief calmed his racing heart but not for long. The Tree of Life's roots shook with rage, its branches slapping against the water. Within moments of the branches and bark blackening, they started to regain their original color again.

"The Tree of Life's regenerating itself!" Ignis exclaimed. "Brace yourself!"

Hundreds of branches rushed at him, violently wrapping their tendrils around his limbs and torso. He squirmed, calling forth Ignis's flames. The roots absorbed the flames, extinguishing them like wisps in the wind. His mana was like a broken vase, emptying out the rest of his strength. His grasp on Ignis weakened, and the sword slipped from his fingers, slapping against the water.

"No, Lucian!" Seraphina screamed, her voice echoing against the cave walls. "Titania, do something!" Glossy tears welled in her eyes.

Lucian's body rapidly was pulled toward The Tree of Life. He braced himself for impact, squeezing his eyes tightly shut. He expected the familiar sensation of bones breaking and blood spilling against rough bark like all of those times with Elias and his goons.

Three...two... one... he internally counted. *What...!*

His body slammed against The Tree of Life, but there was no pain from the impact. He opened his eyes, seeing himself being sucked into the bark. The bark wasn't hard but rather like thick glue or gum. He bit back the urge to scream. He couldn't move. His senses were overflowing with fear, as the branches pulled him inside the trunk. Darkness as he had never seen before shrouded him.

Passing through the soft bark, Lucian was thrust into its core.

He stood up, shivering in complete darkness. His hands instinctively started to rub his arms for warmth. The space that he was in was neither hot nor cold, but the shivers originated from something else—something deeper inside of him that was surfacing.

Waves of emotions flooded into him: fear, regret, hatred, betrayal, and sadness.

An eerily familiar voice broke through the chilling silence. It was a voice that he had only heard once before within the darkest depths of his subconscious. It was a voice that plagued him with his worst fears and deepest regrets.

"*YOU MUST CHOOSE,*" the voice commanded.

"Choose what!" he shouted at the darkness.

The voice replied, with an almost sarcastic tinge to it, "*YOUR FATE.*"

8

TO SAVE A SOUL (PART 2)

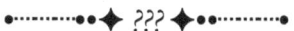 ???

"YOU MUST CHOOSE!" the voice commanded. Wading through the void of darkness, Lucian cried out, "Yeah, yeah, I get it! It's not like you haven't been saying the same thing for the past twenty minutes!"

An endless stretch of darkness greeted him.

A sliver of light finally appeared in the far distance. It twinkled like a star about to be devoured by the surrounding darkness, its brightness rapidly diminishing. He stumbled toward it. As soon as he reached the light, he hit a wall.

Passing through another barrier, Lucian came upon The Tree of Life, but this version was healthy, gifting life to its immediate surroundings through waves of golden light. The Tree of Life's leaves sparkled like rainbow-colored gemstones. The grass lying beneath its umbrella of leaves was the most luscious green that he had ever borne witness to.

But he wouldn't be fooled.

He stood on guard, awaiting whatever this entity had to throw at him.

Slowly but surely, three objects gently emerged out of The Tree of Life's trunk, floating toward him in midair. At first, it was hard for Lucian to fully grasp what was happening. The three objects were shockingly familiar, like the ones he had seen during one of his darkest dreams. They floated side by side, staying close to the bark, which had given birth to them. The golden light wasn't strong enough to eclipse their true auras.

The left object was a dagger, with an ominous, black aura.

The middle object was a rose, with an alluring, red aura.

The right object was a key, with a soothing, silver aura.

Flashes of the hazy, vision-like dream resurfaced. Unlike before, he held firm, not falling for the temptations of any single item. He refused to let himself be guided by foolish curiosity. The urge to grab them was eating into him, but he managed to maintain his composure.

This must be some sort of trick.

Out of the depth of The Tree of Life, the voice repeated itself, "*YOU MUST CHOOSE.*"

What do these things have to do with "my fate?"

In a lighter, softer tone, the voice said, "Child of destiny, who will you choose?"

The objects morphed into larger figures—human figures. The dagger with its sinister aura transformed into Aaron, the rose with its beguiling aura transformed into Seraphina, and the key transformed into two figures, his mother and sister: Lucille and Rosalie. His knees shook at the sight of them, discomfort lodging itself in the back of his throat. His voice cracked, as he called out to each. All of them blankly stared at him, as if their souls had been disconnected from their bodies.

Aaron's figure, bearing the symbol of the dagger, was the first to break the silence by saying, "Looks like the coward has come to seek vengeance."

A crazed look broke the boy's blank expression. He summoned the dagger out of thin air, swinging it maliciously toward Lucian, but he dared not step out of his allotted spot. It was as if all of them were puppets on a string.

Seraphina, bearing the symbol of the rose, was the second to speak. "Lucian, save me! I can't last anymore. Please save me! Hurry before the thorns pierce my throat!"

Out of the abyss, huge, thorny vines wrapped around her. She was like a bird trapped in a cage of death. She reached toward him in desperation and despair.

Lucille's and Rosalie's figures were the final speakers, both bearing the symbol of the key. They spoke in turn. His mother said, "Don't you want to know, my child? I know who and what you are. Trust me, Lucian. Come to me."

Rosalie followed, with a tortured tone, and cried, "Why did you abandon me!"

Lucille's figure was thrown onto the floor, and the life slowly left her eyes. Whereas, Rosalie's figure was tossed from side to side, like a doll, until she eventually lay next to his mother's lifeless body.

As twisted as the scenes were, none of the figures could see each other. They only fixated on Lucian: Aaron mocked him, Seraphina begged him, and Lucille and Rosalie beckoned him. Shortness of breath seized him, tears wetting his face.

This wasn't a choice.

This was hell.

"So, what's your final decision?" the voice re-emerged, relentlessly questioning him. "You only get to choose one —only one."

Rage, anxiety, pain, and sadness overflowed from within.

He felt his head splitting open.

He wanted the pain to stop.

He wanted the hatred to stop.

He wanted the agony to stop.

But he knew that they never would.

After his tear ducts were emptied, a stillness settled over him. He fought against the hysteria seeking to destroy him and surveyed what he saw before him: a fallen comrade, a suffering ally, and the only two people he had ever truly loved. The roads opening before him if he chose each were clear: a path of destruction, a path of salvation, and a path of endless longing and regret. As if to mock him, The Tree of Life allowed Lucian to approach them.

He went to Aaron, his first friend, who had betrayed his trust. He thrust his hand out toward him. Grabbing the dagger with his bare hand, his blood spilled from the freshly made wound. With a strong conviction dripping from his lips, Lucian proclaimed, "I will never lower myself to your level."

He then went past Seraphina, heading to his mother and his half sister. He kissed his mother's forehead, praying with her as the life in her eyes fully left her. He hugged his beaten sister, peace blooming in his heart, as he released her from his grasp. He let her go.

He returned to Seraphina, breaking the thorny vines with his bloodied palms. Without hesitation, he drew her tired figure into his embrace. The Tree of Life recognized his choice, Aaron, Lucille, and Rosalie turning to light and disappearing in the wind. Even Seraphina, who was snugly within his arms, turned to dust and sunk into the earth.

Another figure emerged from The Tree of Life. This one was different. Shining like the sun, a young woman walked toward him with a warm smile settling on her face. As she approached, her golden locks trickled down her body like waves of sunshine. Like the grass surrounding the tree, her green eyes sparkled like fresh dew. She wore a long, white dress with a pattern of flower buds. Her radiance extended beyond the barrier, dispersing the darkness into a sea of light.

"Reincarnation of Morpheus and child of destiny, you have gracefully passed my test," she said with a voice like a light breeze and as soft as a whisper. "I am Vita, the goddess of life and the protector of The Tree of Life."

"Why?" he asked, solemnly. "Why...?"

"Just as Veritas did to Morpheus before you, I gave you three choices. These choices were not only based on your relationships with the people in your life but also your relationships with what they represent—the past, the present, and the future," she explained, the waters parting as she walked. "You chose to move beyond the pains of your past toward a hope-filled future. Lucian, you *are* the one we have been waiting for."

Veritas... Who's that? What is she even talking about?

Vita walked further toward him. The ground beneath her sprung new life with each step. She reached out to him, embracing him in warmth and love. She sang a sweet lullaby, running her fingers through his hair like a mother with her child. "May you find the light and fight for Gaia's life," she whispered into his ear.

Gently releasing him from her embrace, she handed him a vial of liquid that radiated a pure white light. When the vial sat snugly in the palm of his hand, he was whisked out of The Tree of Life's core. He passed through the spongy substance once more, resurfacing in the cave.

A radiant light followed him, The Tree of Life sprouting out fresh buds and returning to its lively state. The barrier broke out of its own accord. Seraphina and Titania ran toward him. He was thrown into an aggressive embrace by Seraphina, who was asking countless questions. A wet sloppy tongue also traveled across his face.

"Guess what I got," he said, proudly.

He held up the vial to Seraphina and Titania.

Titania's fluffy tail wagged, as she said, "You must've met Vita then... Her soul hasn't been fully corrupted, then."

Seraphina tightened her hold on Lucian while saying, "Don't ever do that again, you hear me!" She seemed to be breathing heavily, choking down tears.

Although Lucian had succeeded, the result was nothing more than pure luck. Even so, Lucian learned a valuable lesson: He couldn't let his future be dictated by his past.

•··········•✦ *Bluewater* ✦•··········•

WHILE LUCIAN'S HEAD WAS IN THE CLOUDS, THE group arrived at The Broken Latch. Seraphina led the way toward the front door, but she abruptly stopped walking, causing Lucian to almost knock her over. All of the illumination crystals inside the shop were strangely unlit, the door was left ajar, and there were large cracks in the windows.

Without any hesitation, Seraphina burst through the front door. Lucian and Titania raced after her, heading inside the shop. The interior fared far worse than the exterior.

The illumination crystals had been smashed into tiny pieces, the wooden desks were broken into several halves, and the broken locks riddled the floorboards. Dark stains were seeping into the wooden floor. A wretched stench filled Lucian's nostrils, which he attributed to the black liquid running along the lines of the floorboards. He watched as Seraphina violently shook, stifling a scream. Leon was nowhere in sight.

Titania raced toward the back of the store, calling them to her. Lucian and Seraphina joined Titania in one of the guest rooms. The black liquid and stains on the floorboards matched the blood-like substance painted on the walls of the guest room. It spelled out something in the ancient language.

"*THE HARVESTING HAS BEGUN*" was inscribed in bold letters, the grotesque black liquid dripping onto the floorboards beneath the message.

Titania seemed to be unfazed, as she said, "It's a little earlier than expected, but we need to leave Bluewater, *now*."

"And go where!?" Seraphina cried out, hysterically. "We can't leave without Leon! Let's wait until we find him first!"

Titania said, in a serious and sharp tone, "Leon won't die that easily, so don't worry. The attackers are after Lucian, and you know what'll happen if they find him. Now, get packed quickly. We're leaving immediately."

Seraphina, like a fire doused in oil, stormed out of the room to pack her belongings. Lucian remained to pack since, unfortunately, this bloody mess was his room.

Titania seemed to be lost in her thoughts, as Lucian asked, "Where are we headed, Titania?"

Titania drew in a long breath before saying, "I'm taking you to the one place where I know you'll be safe... The Terras Empire."

9

A FATEFUL ENCOUNTER

Two weeks had passed since the start of their travels to The Terras Empire. For the most part, the trip was peaceful, as the roads had been all but abandoned. What traveler would want to visit a cursed empire with little to no chance of entry? Because there was a slight likelihood of running into their pursuers, the trio needed to travel as covertly as possible.

As such, Seraphina rented out a merchant's carriage and chose aliases for them. Seraphina assigned herself the role of a fabric merchant, who was delivering goods to a moderately well-known Terrasian clothing brand, *Tanzanite Threads*. Lucian assumed the role of a mercenary hired to protect the precious wares. Since Titania was more of a pet than a person, she simply pretended like she couldn't speak.

Throughout most of their travels, the sky stayed crystal clear. Occasionally, however, tiny, fluffy clouds floated in the ocean of blue like marshmallows. The weather was pleasant as well—the warm winds comforting their more chilling circumstances. Terrifying images of The Broken Latch kept resurfacing in Lucian's head, throwing his emotions in and out of turmoil. These conflicted feelings of uncertainty and guilt churned in his stomach, making him anxious about Leon, his savior turned ally.

A grimace settled on his face.

Seraphina, who was driving the carriage, turned her head slightly to look at him. When their eyes met, a strange expression formed on her face.

"Just looking at you makes me feel depressed." She jested. "Cheer up, Lucian. If anyone can beat the odds, it's Leon. Besides, what else can I do for him but hope for his safety?"

Ah, that's right. Leon is like a father to Seraphina. She's the one who's feeling the weight of his disappearance and the destruction of her home more than anyone.

In a mock jester, Lucian slapped his face with both of his palms, hitting himself a little *too* hard. It stung like a boot to the face, but he bore the pain. As Seraphina's friend, Lucian resolved to be in good spirits, so she wouldn't have to worry about him too. Seraphina seemed shocked by his sudden action but also relieved—evident by the cute dimples appearing on her face, which always showed themselves when she smiled or laughed.

"Alright, you two lovebirds," Titania teased, "We're getting closer to our destination, so you need to stay focused."

"We'll be fine," Lucian said. "We haven't run into any problems yet."

"*Yet*," Titania repeated his words back to him.

Completely ignoring her teasing, Lucian sarcastically remarked, "You sound like we're walking into a den of starving Lychnuses."

"We might as well be," Titania scoffed, jumping from the inside of the arched carriage to the spot in between Lucian and Seraphina at the front. "The road we need to travel on isn't nicknamed 'Ambush Alley' for nothing. Normally, we would've traveled by boat to avoid it, but as you know, all sea travel has been cut off on The Terras Empire's end."

Reaching his hand into the carriage, Lucian ferreted through his belongings and retrieved an old and weathered map. Untying the string that held the parchment together like a scroll, Lucian flattened the map out on his lap. His eyes surveyed the listed road names. The names were hand-written, so some of them were illegible, but fortunately, he could piece together the true name of "Ambush Alley."

"Marlais Road," he read, minding his pronunciation. "Why does that name ring a bell...Marlais?"

Seraphina momentarily peeked at the map, as she explained, "I knew you were isolated from the outside world but not to this extent. Marlais is the surname of The Terras Empire's Royal Family."

Seraphina clutched the reins tighter and steered the horses slightly to the right to avoid an oncoming carriage, as she explained, "Essentially, The Terrasian Emperor was usurped and killed several years ago. Now, all that's left of his legacy is this dingy road."

Ignoring the dead emperor and focusing on the present, Lucian asked, "Well, what are we supposed to do if we're ambushed on our way through 'Ambush Alley?'" Lucian resigned himself to an inevitable run-in with bandits.

"Nothing," Titania said, almost stoically. "Our top priority is to get you into The Terras Empire without drawing suspicion to ourselves. As long as they don't kidnap or kill you, they're free to take whatever they want. If they attempt either, I'll distract them long enough for you and Seraphina to escape. She will have to guide you the rest of the way there. It's that important to Evangeline to deliver you *safely*."

"But what about you!" Lucian exclaimed. "Even though you can use magic and handle yourself, you're still, well, a small creature. You'd have to fight dangerous, armed men."

Reassuringly, she placed the light-pink soft pads of her paw on his hand and said, "Don't underestimate me, child. With my power alone, I could take down at least ten of them."

While they had been leisurely chatting away, the once vibrant environment immediately changed. What had been a pleasant ride on a nicely paved path and through bright and healthy trees turned into a dark, chilly road with an almost stagnant atmosphere and dead leaves.

The only comparison that Lucian could think of was the changing of seasons. Over the past few weeks, it was like spring, but now, it was like the harshest months of winter. While there was no snow to indicate the winter season, a deep fog formed, hanging low along the base of the dirt path. The once bright trees were now a hollow gray color, and their leaves rustled eerily from the cutting wind that blew through them. The drop in temperature caused his teeth to chatter.

I can see why it's called "Ambush Alley," he joked to himself, trying to lighten his rapidly sinking mood.

Surprisingly, they managed to travel halfway down the passage without even a glimpse of a bandit or another life form. The absence of an attack seemed to lull Lucian and Seraphina into a false sense of security. However, Titania stayed on high alert, each rustle of a nearby tree making her fur needle upward. This pattern continued for an hour. Lucian tried to keep his wits about him, but his mind was in a trance. Even when the noises from the wind became like whispers in his ears, and the crunch of dead leaves under the horses' hooves became like the crushing of brittle bones, Lucian was mentally tired enough to drift into a sleep.

As soon as Lucian completely let his guard down, as if on cue, a band of dark silhouettes appeared in front of the carriage holding what seemed to be a collection of spears or long swords. Lucian's eyes flicked toward Titania, whose tail was spiked upward.

Seraphina looked as if she was trying to find a way around the bandits, but to no avail. The road was completely straight with rows of trees on either end, so there was no way to weave around the attackers with a horse-drawn carriage. Even if they forced their way through the line of bandits, their carriage would sustain considerable damage. Escaping through the trees wasn't even an option since the gaps in between them were too small for a carriage. Escaping on foot also wasn't a smart idea since there was still too much road left until they reached the entrance of the empire. Turning around wasn't a choice at all, for she knew what monsters awaited them if they returned to Avrith. In the end, they had no choice but to head straight into danger. Lucian drew in a sharp breath, cursing his bad luck once again.

Titania retreated to the inside of the carriage and whispered to him, "Remember what I told you. Don't engage unless absolutely necessary. One more thing, if you hear me say, 'We really need to deliver this package,' then run."

Lucian reluctantly nodded.

Seraphina's carriage came to an abrupt stop as the bandits pointed their weapons at them. Much to Lucian's surprise, the bandits weren't what he had expected. They looked closer to beggars than bandits with their gaunt figures, muddied clothes, and scarred hands.

They were without a doubt Terrasians, as their features closely matched Aaron's. However, unlike Aaron, the way that they brandished their weapons was amateurish. They weren't the evil menaces Lucian had envisioned... It honestly would've been better if they were. That would've made it easier to despise them. Their eyes were nearly lifeless but not completely dead, and they had deep bags underneath them.

From the end of the line came a scrawny male, who looked to be only a child of ten or eleven years old. His teeth were cracked, his eyes were dull, his frame was dangerously thin, and his arms were shaking. He had the same scared facial expression as Silas Elwood during his Succession Ceremony many moons ago.

With a wavering voice, the boy demanded, "G-Give me all yer goods." He inched toward the front of the carriage, pointing the spear in Lucian's direction. "O-Or else yer get it!"

"Alright," Lucian replied with a firm voice. "So long as you'll spare our lives, you can take whatever you want from the carriage."

A flash of guilt appeared on the boy's face, but that expression soon turned into pride, because he succeeded in what looked like his first robbery. He hastened to the carriage, desperately grabbing at any leftover food and valuable belongings. While the boy successfully stole from the carriage, he forgot to check Lucian and Seraphina for any valuables on their persons. It looked like the boy was lost in his own little world.

Several more boys started to loot, while the adult bandits formed a full circle around the carriage to completely encircle the trio. One of the adult bandits left the line and approached them. In both appearance and aura, he was different from the child who robbed the carriage like a small bird desperate for a crumb. This man was the bulkiest of the bandits with pitch-black hair and scars on his face and body. He held an enormous, scary-looking sword in his hand.

"Apologies for our youngin'. He's like a newborn faun, ya understand?" The man spoke up, letting a laugh escape his mouth. "Ya folks, it looks like ya have more than ya let on. Come 'ere and let us inspect yer clothes for the rest."

Compliantly, Lucian and Seraphina slowly slid off their seats and approached the leader, stopping at a reasonable distance. Kidnapping was the worst-case scenario, after all. If only the leader had told them to throw their belongings on the ground, they would've had no problem. It was as if he read their thoughts. The leader walked toward them, getting close enough to spit on them. Starting with Lucian, the leader personally seized his belongings.

Naturally, the leader disarmed Lucian first, taking Ignis away. Lucian was so focused on losing Ignis that he forgot about the other items. Master Felix's scepter and notebook, Eva's ring, the vial from The Tree of Life, and Melinda's Credit Slip were violently seized. The notebook was dirty-looking, and the vial seemed like medicine, so the leader seemed to ignore them, but the ring, the scepter, and the Credit Slip caught his greedy eye.

"Simon, this is what ya get fer slackin', boy!" the leader

exclaimed, pointing the child out of the crowd. "Look at all of these treasures that ya skipped over!"

A sense of panic spread across Lucian's face. He couldn't afford to lose his sword, scepter, or ring. All of them held considerable value. Subconsciously, he moved his hand toward the items to retrieve them, but it was too late.

No, no, no, don't touch that!

As if the ring heard Lucian's desperate pleas, the moment that the leader's fingers touched the band, waves of electricity shot out of it. The leader quickly pulled his hand away, a deep, purple bruise bubbling from the skin around the injury. Lucian couldn't believe his eyes, but the ring really rejected the bandit. The leader cursed in his native tongue, shooting Lucian a deadly glare. He eyed the ring a few more times, but he decided to leave the cursed item on the ground to rust.

However, another problem arose.

"Look what I found!" one of the bandits exclaimed from behind them.

Holding her upside down by the tail, the bandit had captured Titania from inside the carriage. While the group of boys had overlooked her due to their hunger, this bandit seemingly found pleasure in torturing a seemingly small, helpless creature.

Lucian looked at Seraphina, whose eyes sent a murderous gleam in the bandit's direction.

"Let her go," she grumbled, her fingernails digging into the skin of her palms.

Indignantly, the bandit taunted her by saying, "What's a little girl like ya gonna do 'bout it?"

Too busy nursing his injured hand, the leader had neglected to take Seraphina's weapon away. Quickly, from her cloak, she retrieved her wand. With a flick of her wrist and a verbal incantation, she cast a spell, causing several rocks to strike the bandit's hand. He grimaced in pain, releasing Titania's tail.

Landing on her paws, Titania sprinted to Lucian and Seraphina, reciting the code words. "We really need to deliver this package," she ordered, snarling through her teeth.

To the surprise of the bandits and even to her own companions, Titania amassed an incredible amount of mana in her body. Her entire body started to glow. Not even a minute after, she released the mana, an explosion of light blinding the bandits. Although Lucian and Seraphina weren't familiar with Titania's powers, they sensed her accumulating mana far before the bandits.

Shielding his eyes with his arm, Lucian took the opportunity to snatch his stolen belongings. Seraphina had already sprinted toward safety, and he intended to follow her. But something, no, someone was preventing him. Even among the cursing and shouting of the bandits, who blindly groped the air, the young bandit tenaciously held on to him. While Lucian previously pitied him, the boy was now a huge thorn in his side—an annoying anchor preventing his escape.

The boy was latched onto Lucian's ankle for dear life with his eyes scrunched closed. Lucian didn't want to harm him, so he resorted to flailing his leg around, trying to shake him off. Luckily, it didn't take much force for the small boy's grip to fail. Unfortunately, the time wasted while Lucian attempted to break free was just enough for the leader to locate him when the light fully faded. The leader tackled him to the ground. The leader's knee was positioned on the back of Lucian's neck, trying to suffocate him.

Seraphina had fled far into the distance, only realizing Lucian wasn't behind her when the explosion of light had fully fizzled out. Her screams echoed throughout the trees, calling his name in desperation. Even though Seraphina started to chant another incantation, Lucian knew that her magic couldn't help him from that distance. Seraphina's magic, unfortunately, had a restricted range of effects. Titania couldn't help him either, as she had been seized by a different bandit. Her mana reserves appeared to be completely drained from her previous spell.

Adding more and more pressure, the leader said, "Thought ya could get 'way, now, did'ya? Too bad I couldn't grab your girlfriend instead."

Lucian's silence seemed to confuse the leader. With as much force as the leader was applying to his knee, any adult man in this situation would've been suffocating. However, Lucian lay still, as if he were unaffected. Unbeknownst to the leader, Lucian was continuously protected by a divine shield, Aerus. At some point, the leader bent his head down to look at Lucian's face. Instead of clenched teeth or tearful eyes, Lucian's face expressed a silent rage.

I've been holding back for Titania's sake, but this bandit's getting on my last nerve.

"You have two choices," Lucian said. "Get your knee off my neck or else."

"Or else, what?" The leader crudely laughed.

Immediately, the pressure of the leader's knee on Lucian's neck was forcibly removed. Lucian rose from the ground, looking around completely confused, as he hadn't even made his move yet. To the right of him, Lucian heard a loud *crunch*! The burly man who was once on top of him had been thrown straight into a tree by an overwhelming force.

Surveying the scene, Lucian realized that the rest of the bandits had been subdued, too.

With a hearty laugh, a familiar man's voice proclaimed,

"Fancy meeting you here, kid. I always knew we'd see each other again, but certainly not like this!"

Dropping his mouth open, Lucian shouted in disbelief, "D-Darius!?"

"Ha! Ha! Ha! Yes, it is I, Darius Grindenwald!" the man exclaimed, proudly pointing his sword up into the air. "The one-and-only Captain of The Royal Guards is at your service."

10

THE TERRAS EMPIRE

 *Marlais Road*

What a curious-looking ring," Darius said, as he tried to pick it up from the ground. "And these unique engravings... Hm, quite the sight to see."

Like when the bandit's leader touched the ring, Darius received an electric shock.

"The bandits thought the same thing when they decided to loot it from me," Lucian stated, retrieving the ring and stuffing it back into his pocket.

"Ha! Ha! Of course, of course! I apologize..." Darius slightly bowed his head, but his eyes seemed to have a glint of unbridled curiosity within them. "Surely, such a rare treasure should be kept close to its rightful owner."

Seraphina approached the pair and said, "Excuse me for interrupting, but I think the bandits may wake up any time now, so could we please move this conversation to a safer location?"

Darius's attention turned to Seraphina for the first time, and he looked amused. "No need to worry," he assured her, lowering his gaze to meet hers. "I used my mana and enough physical force to knock them unconscious until tomorrow, *at the very least*. That, I can assure you. Although, on another note, may I ask why you're headed to The Terras Empire?"

Before either Lucian or Seraphina could reply, Titania brushed herself against Lucian's leg. "Don't draw too much attention...is what I want to say, but it's too late. I don't know how you know The Captain of The Royal Guards, but we can't allow him to question us too much and potentially report us to his superiors. Tell him that we're delivering a package to a trusted buyer," she warned, telepathically.

Her eyes were dead serious, so Lucian followed her instructions without question. Even without telepathic communication, Seraphina seemed to understand the gist of the unspoken exchange between Titania and Lucian and decided to take matters into her own hands.

She swiftly replied, "We have a buyer in The Terras Empire who requested fabrics and sewing materials to buy at a bulk price. Entrance into and exit out of The Terras Empire is restricted to outsiders, but we have brought an official permit to allow for this transaction."

From within her cloak, she pulled out a long, rectangular wooden tablet with the words, "*Verified Universal Trader*," written in a bold font.

Darius had an impressed look on his face, but it didn't seem to be the tablet itself that he was interested in. Many years of observing his father and the villagers made Lucian certain of the man's fake expression.

The captain's interest lay in Seraphina herself. He was clearly analyzing her. Lucian grew worried for Seraphina's safety, directing the conversation elsewhere. Cracking a few jokes here and there and then flailing like a fish, he managed to direct Darius's attention back to him.

"This is perfect timing, though," Darius remarked, with a lively tone. "I was actually heading back anyway, so let me accompany you to your destination."

"It's alright, we—" Seraphina stated, attempting to decline his offer.

"Don't be silly!" Darius proclaimed, patting her head like one would a child. "I don't see a good reason for you to refuse my offer. There's no better bodyguard than yours truly, The Captain of The Royal Guards!"

"If you insist," Seraphina caved.

With Darius riding his horse at the fore, Lucian,

Seraphina, and Titania followed in their carriage. Lucian watched as the unconscious bodies of the bandits disappeared farther and farther down the road, eventually looking like tiny fleas in the distance. He was grateful for Darius rescuing them, but he had a creeping feeling of discomfort. He didn't know why, but he was disturbed at the way that Darius had stared at Seraphina previously.

After thirty minutes had passed, Darius slowed his horse's pace to a full stop. Seraphina simultaneously tightened her grip on the horse's reins and halted the carriage, too. At the end of the dirt pathway, known as "Marlais Road," a ginormous metallic gate with weapons perched on the very top stood. Several soldiers seemed to be stationed at key locations along the wall and were on high alert. Some manned the weapons, others surveyed the area, and a few stood near the lever that opened and closed the gates.

From the top, one of the soldiers shouted, "State your name and reason for entrance."

With a voice like thunder, Darius exclaimed, "Darius Grindenwald has returned from his monthly expedition along with three traveling companions. Let us pass!" His voice alone left no doubt of his authority or identity.

"Permission for entry granted! Mind your distance from the wall!" the soldier warned, signaling the other soldiers to open the gate.

The whole ground shook as the gate scraped open. The screeching of the metal rang in Lucian's ears such that he reflexively cupped them with his hands. His eyes were squeezed shut to prevent dust particles from clouding and irritating them.

When the gate fully opened, Lucian reopened his eyes to a horrifying sight. A dark mist seeped out of the gates, looking like spindly fingers reaching out to touch him. He gulped down his displeasure as he watched Darius casually ride through the gate with ease. Seraphina appeared to have a similar reaction to his, but she didn't let her sentiments show for long. From her mouth, she let out a sharp whistle, signaling the horses to lurch forward.

Once or twice, Darius looked back at the carriage and locked eyes with him. The captain's eyes conveyed amusement, while Lucian's eyes conveyed distress. About a few minutes into the thickest part of the mist, a foul stench rose from the sewers and into Lucian's nostrils. He hoarsely coughed, swinging his cloak over his nose and mouth to try to lessen the unwelcome intrusion. He soon realized that the mist wasn't just from the sewers but from the entirety of the town. There was no way to escape it. Even with Master Felix's talisman and his familiarity with The Fallen District, this smell was on a whole other level.

At a few intervals, the mist's thickness thinned out enough to let him stake out the area. With what little vision he had, Lucian saw a multitude of dilapidated houses, or what were in the general shape of houses, at the very least. The streets were littered with liquid waste, black and brown sludge overflowing from the crevices in the cobblestone.

He swore that he wouldn't disembark from the carriage even if someone told him to. It was like the disease had completely ravaged the entire town, leaving nothing more than toxic waste in its wake. The few inhabitants of this godless town that he did see were nothing more than skeletons aimlessly walking.

"What is this place?" he whispered to Seraphina, in between coughs. "This place is even worse than The Fallen District in Caelum."

"Sadly, ninety percent of The Terras Empire is in this state," Seraphina whispered back to him. "The rumors are reality, after all."

Lucian noticed that Seraphina didn't seem to be suffering from the stench. "W-Why aren't you affected?"

Like a master speaking to her student, she said, "I'm using a purification spell, Lucian. Gather as much mana as you can into your face, envision the purest thing that you can think of, and then say, '*Mundare.*' It's actually a more difficult process than my explanation, but I trust that your *exceptional* skills will allow you to do it easily. Now, stop whining."

"What if I can't!?" Lucian complained. "I'm going to die if I inhale anymore."

"Stop being so dramatic. You won't die," she stated, rolling her eyes. "I think..."

"Great, thanks, Seraphina."

Gathering as much mana into his face as he possibly could, Lucian conjured images of the spring near The Sage's Forest in Caelum. Next, he recited the word, "*Mundare.*" The purification spell activated, creating a thin film over his face. The stench filtered through the film, transforming the particles into a nice, refreshing scent.

•···········••✦ *Blackridge* ✦••···········•

WHEN THEY REACHED THE CAPITAL CITY, Blackridge, Lucian was too tired to even react. Although activating the purification spell was easy enough, constantly maintaining a "pure image" inside his head was the issue. He had to reapply the magic not once, not twice, but ten times!

Noticing a shift in the air, Lucian realized that the dark clouds and thick mist cleared out before him. Blackridge was sunny with a light, refreshing breeze. Not one dilapi-dated building was in sight, but instead, multiple gleaming, shiny houses and shops stretched out into infinity. The buildings looked to be made of some of the same materials as the outer gate, which sparkled magnificently in the sunlight.

Thousands of capital dwellers roamed the cobblestone streets shopping, socializing, and selling. They donned glamorous clothes and were well-fed. The men wore royal-purple tunics lined with accents of silver and extravagant hats, while the women wore ocean-blue dresses with accents of maroon and radiant jewels adorning their heads.

Unlike the stigma that came with their natural features in other kingdoms, Lucian found their behavior not any different from the inhabitants of Lunaris, Avrith, or Caelum. People were people, no matter their outward appearance.

Darius broke the silence and said, "It looks like we'll have to part ways here, as I'm headed to the palace to submit a report. The gods have blessed this meeting and will bless many more! Let us meet again one day, hopefully very soon."

With that, Darius disappeared into the crowd. A sense of relief washed over Lucian as he watched the boisterous captain ride away in the opposite direction of where they were headed. Titania finally resurfaced from the inside of the carriage, giving Seraphina directions here and there, when needed, careful not to draw any attention to them. At times, Titania even made a few animal noises to deceive anyone who even so much as looked in their direction.

Along the way to their destination, Lucian noticed that the capital dwellers, while better dressed and fed than their poorer counterparts, looked no happier than them. They wore masks of fake smiles with hollow eyes looking onward into an unknown oblivion.

Almost like they were in a trance.

Something felt off about the capital.

While he was lost in his thoughts, they had arrived at their destination. Seraphina hopped off the carriage and tied the horses to a wooden post, while Titania headed toward the front of the establishment. Out of all the buildings in Blackridge, this one looked by far the most rundown.

It appeared to be made of a more brittle-looking material than the shimmering stones, and its windows were clouded with dirt. But as he knew from previous experiences, such as Master Maverick's shop, he decided to forgo his judgment based solely on outward appearance.

Titania went inside first, entering through a narrow opening at the base of the door perfectly sized for a small animal. Seraphina entered next, with Lucian following her. Upon entering the building, he took a quick glance around, not too impressed by what he saw. Unlike with the other shops, there was no surprise reveal. They had entered a house—plain and simple. The interior mirrored that of a humble home in Caelum, much like his own. The furniture and decorations were scarce. Everything was wooden with a slow-burning fireplace on the left-hand side.

"Is this a joke?" Lucian asked, disappointingly.

Titania interrupted his premature brooding and said, "Not everything is what it appears to be—"

"—And not everyone is who they seem to be," a mysterious but soothing voice said, finishing Titania's statement.

Out of the back room came an elderly woman with familiar features. Although her hair was white as snow, her locks retained a certain shimmer. Her lips had a deep rouge painted on them, and her eyes glistened like gold. Even her angelic voice rang knowingly in his ears. A look of confusion crossed his face, while Titania and Seraphina seemed unperturbed by the voice's owner. The woman approached him, her dainty hands gently resting on his face. The crinkles near her eyes, when she smiled, were familiar too.

"Who are you?" Lucian blurted out, his mind trying to make sense of the dissonance.

Winking her right eye and pinching his cheek, she said, "For Felix's student, you're not very bright, are you, Lucian?"

A pang of realization hit him.

The words flowed out of his mouth like a flood, "E-Eva, is that really you!?"

A spark of excitement flashed in his eyes.

"Why, yes, I am, Lucian," Eva confirmed. "Why, yes, I am."

II

THE PLAN

Blackridge

E va led them to a study room deeper inside her house. As they walked down a long hall, Lucian was back in his thoughts. Although Leon already said that she didn't die back in Lunaris, it still took him some time to adjust to her presence and her true form. As a master of illusionary magic, it made sense that she could disguise her outer appearance at will, but it didn't lessen his awe seeing the transformation firsthand.

By the time that he had wrapped his head around the situation, they arrived at the study room. Like the lock systems used in Caelum, the study room had a mana-sensitive sensor synced to recognize Eva and her designated guests. She rested her palm on the sensor, infusing it with her mana. With a quick click, the door automatically swung open, as if it were ushering them into the room. The study room had a quaint feel to it, matching the interior design of the living room at the front of the house. Unlike the living room, however, there lay strategically placed magical items disguised as regular household decorations.

Eva took her place, sitting behind the mahogany desk located at the back of the room, signaling for them to approach her. From the stack of papers cluttering the top of her desk, she singled one out, bringing it to Lucian's attention.

He retrieved the paper from her, analyzing its contents. It seemed to be a hand-drawn, rough sketch of a structure's blueprints with poorly written handwriting labeling the entry and exit points, as well as any important names of specific rooms. Unlike the other papers on her desk, this specific one was creased horribly and had several sections blotted out with ink stains. Even so, he meticulously looked at every little detail, no matter how insignificant it may be.

Handing the blueprints back, he asked, "Is the Alliance of The Fallen getting a new headquarters or something?"

Shaking her head, she said, "No, this is what our

undercover operative, Lorin, has been diligently working on for the last year and a half. She infiltrated the palace as a maid, listing as many possible infiltration and escape routes for our next major operation."

"It's been a year and a half, so why is it still incomplete?" Lucian asked.

Creases formed on Eva's forehead as she explained, "In her last letter of correspondence, she expressed fears that she was under suspicion by one of her supervisors, and so she sent this rough sketch to me. The missing parts were supposed to be delivered later as she gained access to those areas, but they never arrived. It's been about two months since her last letter, so I can only assume she's been taken prisoner in the palace. Lawrence volunteered to go, but…"

"Why not send that Lawrence fellow in Lorin's place?" Lucian asked.

"Aside from the head butler and The Royal Guards, men are scarce in the palace," Eva explained. "While I would've loved to send another female operative to take Lorin's place, we're severely short-staffed. The Royal Guards have whittled down our numbers over the years."

"How many of you are there?"

"For the last few months, it's only been me, Lawrence, and Lorin…"

An awkward silence filled the study.

"If you just need another female, then surely I could fill her role?" Seraphina suggested, a bright fire of passion burning in her eyes.

Lucian was impressed by Seraphina's bravery, but even though her tone of voice was steady, he could see a flicker of fear hidden beneath the passionate flames.

"As much as I admire your resolve to finish these blueprints, the maid selection process has ended for this year," Eva stated. "On top of that, our adversaries seem to have anticipated our efforts, especially with Lorin's recent disappearance. Entry into the palace is more difficult than ever before. The only ones allowed unrestricted movement, in and out of the palace, are members of The Royal Guards..."

"Darius," Lucian mumbled under his breath.

"That's why I took the initiative to bring you to Terras, Lucian," Eva explained.

"Right into the lion's den?"

"As crazy as it sounds, The Terras Empire is the safest place for you. The Soulless were tracking you very closely. So close, in fact, that they narrowed down your location to somewhere in Avrith, after momentarily losing you in The Talis Mountains," she explained. "Leon and I were in constant contact, and we planned everything in advance. During the raid of The Broken Latch, I fabricated a pseudo-human, illusionary version of you. The 'fake you' escaped with Leon, taking them off *your* actual trail. The Soulless must've already caught onto my little trick, but it bought you enough time to cross into The Terras Empire unharmed. Since it's the base of our operations, ATF's headquarters has the best security. I can protect you here."

He lowered his head, taking it all in. "Why didn't you or Leon just tell me? Even more importantly, why didn't you explain anything to Seraphina?"

Eva diverted her attention to Seraphina and shot her an apologetic look while saying, "I'm sorry for keeping you in the dark, but you'll just have to trust me for now."

Interlocking her hands, she said, "There's actually another reason why I wanted you to come to The Terras Empire... I need you to join The Royal Guards."

Lucian felt as if a wave violently crashed into him. He couldn't process her words. A loud buzzing noise muffled his ears. "I'm sorry, what did you just say? Can you repeat that again?"

Cracking a light joke, she said, "You know what they always say, 'There's no better cover than hiding in plain sight.'"

"To protect me, you want to throw me into enemy territory. How does that make any sense?" he asked, his voice spiking. "What about that Lawrence guy? He's one of the Terrasian operatives, too, isn't he? Isn't he a hundred times more prepared for the job than I am? I can't follow your line of thinking, Eva. Besides, The Captain of The Royal Guards, Darius, and The Vice Captain, Angelique, both know what I look like! I saw Darius on the way here!"

"To answer your first question, Lawrence is a highly skilled operative, but he has a fatal weakness: his twin sister, *Lorin*. The moment that he enters the palace, he'd abandon his mission and search for her," she sighed while saying. "To answer your second question, concealing your true identity is easier than you think. Did you already forget that I can use illusionary magic?"

For the first time since the conversation started, Titania piped up and countered, "While I can't say I understand your plan, Eva, I do trust you. However, I doubt that The Royal Guards would allow just anyone to join their ranks, let alone be fooled by a simple illusion spell. You, of all people, know that Lucian is distinguished by more than just his physical features. While unable to fully control his mana, the sheer density of it is enough to alert anyone who can sense mana. It'll be even easier for The Royal Guards to detect his identity with their skills."

Eva tightened her hands, blowing a loose strand of white hair out of her face. "I understand your concerns, but it's not like we've been twiddling our thumbs here in Terras for the past two years," she said, firmly. "I expected them to be a problem, even if Lucian wasn't involved in any of our missions. Before he arrived, I prepared a special accessory that he can use to monitor and adjust his mana outflow as well as conceal his identity."

Reaching inside her desk, Eva retrieved a small, black box from a concealed compartment. She handed the box to Lucian, who reluctantly accepted the gift. He opened the box to find a pair of earrings with clear jewels embedded in them.

The moment that he touched one of them, the color turned murky. He retracted his finger, and the color turned clear again. He tested the earrings, finding that the more mana he infused into the jewels, the more opaque the colors became. He reluctantly clasped them in his ears.

"You'll get used to them soon enough," Eva assured him. "I tried making them as light as possible since it can be uncomfortable wearing them over long periods of time."

He ignored her, continuing to test their capabilities. Drowning out the sound of Eva's voice even further, he realized that the color wasn't the only thing that changed when he infused mana into the jewels. The more mana he infused, the slower his mana refilled in his body. Once he felt like he was getting the hang of using them, he returned to listening to her. But, in those few minutes of slacking concentration, he missed more than he had thought.

"I don't think Lucian was listening at all, unfortunately," Seraphina tattled.

"Yes, it seems so," Eva agreed. "I guess I'll just have to go over it one more time. Lucian, are you listening, now?"

"Even if I was, the whole plan is insane," Lucian muttered.

Eva pretended to ignore his comment and explained, "The Royal Guards are always on the lookout for promising new members. They don't discriminate on race, gender, age, or status, so they're popular with the Terrasian citizens. The only thing that they care about is power. So, here is where you come in, Lucian. Unlike other organizations that require years of experience or a special recommendation, The Royal Guards hold a mini tournament or tryout once a month to determine the individual strengths of their applicants. All you need to do is win three matches in total to qualify for the bottom ranks. Depending on your performance, you could be placed anywhere from the bottom ranks, which consist of everyday soldiers; the middle ranks, which consist of bodyguards to high-ranking officials; and the high ranks, which consist of the top ten strongest members, including Captain Darius and Vice-Captain Angelique."

"So, let's say I go along with this outlandish plan. What rank do you need me to shoot for?" he asked, his curiosity growing. "I'm confident enough to get into the bottom ranks, but I don't think I can reach the high ranks. Even during my fight with Angelique at The Battle of the

Bronze in Korakk, I realized that she was holding back her true power. If I try to reach the high ranks during the tournament, I might draw Darius's attention and accidentally expose myself."

"I'm impressed with how much your thinking has matured," Eva praised him. "I want you to reach the middle ranks. The middle ranks usually protect the officials who work in the palace, so you would have the most access, in and out of it. Although the high ranks have access to all of the areas of the palace, they are based out of a separate building in Blackridge, so it may arouse too much suspicion if you keep requesting to go to the palace without a reason."

"So, when is this tournament being held?" he asked, a strange feeling of nervousness creeping up his throat. "I do need time to prepare for it, don't I?"

"Hmm... Well, striking the iron when it's hot is most effective, so I hate to inform you like this, but the tournament starts tomorrow. As soon as I discerned that you safely entered Terras, I sent Lawrence to submit your application to participate." Eva gave him a mischievous smile while practically signing his death certificate. "But don't worry! Lawrence will help you with all of your preparations and explain to you the more specific details of this mission. He's one of our most skilled undercover operatives, so you should be fi—"

From behind them, the study door flew open with even more gusto than when they had entered. A young man rushed into the room, forgoing any semblance of courtesy or manners. His shoulder-length, messy black hair and bark-colored eyes matched those of any other Terrasian; however, he was significantly taller and slimmer than the ones Lucian had seen on the streets. He gave off an air of impatience and rage as he scowled the moment his eyes linked with Lucian's.

"Is this puny shrimp really going to be my replacement!?" he shouted at Eva. "I told you I could handle this mission, and yet you hand it over to some dimwitted amateur."

Eva released a long sigh and then addressed his heated words. "Lawrence, mind your manners. You already know why I can't send you on this mission. Even with your skills, you become a complete mess when Lorin is involved. I can't leave such an important task to someone who is too emotionally involved. This isn't a game, child."

Slamming his fists onto her desk, Lawrence looked even more aggravated as he angrily protested, "I refuse to leave my twin sister's life in the hands of some stranger!"

"He's not some stranger!" Eva raised her voice, a small fire sparking in her eyes.

Sticking his chin in the air, he mocked her while saying, "Ah, yes, of course. This is The Regulus, the holy prophetic child we've been waiting for all of these years. Take a good look at him and at our situation, Eva! Where was he when The Terras Empire fell into the hands of a corrupt force? Where was he when seventy-five percent of our forces were wiped out during our last operation? Probably still in his rural village, completely unaware of our sacrifices."

Lawrence let out a cruel snicker, eyes glaring with spite.

The end was quick.

Lucian heard flesh hitting flesh. Eva's hand slapped Lawrence's face in a matter of a few seconds. Everyone in the room, especially Lucian, was too shocked to immediately react. Once the embers settled and the standoff came to its breaking point, Lawrence stormed out in a huff.

Eva collected herself and sat back down in her chair. "I apologize for his behavior. I have raised him and his sister ever since they were young. I must've spoiled him too much."

"You don't need to apologize," Lucian said with firm assurance. "In my opinion, it's much better to spare the rod and spoil the child. At least, that's what I would've wanted."

"You're right, Lucian," Eva said, appearing deep in her thoughts. "You're dismissed for today. I told you as much as you need to know for this mission. Tomorrow, I'll get Lawrence to help you, no matter what."

Lucian, Seraphina, and Tatiana retreated to the spare guest rooms in the house. As soon as he entered his room, he jumped onto the bed headfirst. When his face hit the pillow, he fell straight asleep. Even though he wasn't too thrilled with Eva's plan, at least a nice, warm bed was way better than the wooden base of the carriage.

12

THE ROYAL GUARDS

 *Blackridge*

When Lucian woke up, he found several items lying right outside his door: a change of clothes, a fake identification card, and an appearance-altering bracelet. Seeing everything was perfectly prepared for his mission, it was apparent that Eva wasn't taking "no" for an answer. Even without his explicit consent, his fate was already decided for him...*again*.

Reluctantly collecting the items off the wooden floor, he returned to his room. Before he put anything on, he placed all of the items that he had received from Eva on the bed and closely inspected them. Already having tested the earrings the day prior, the focus of his examination was the appearance-altering bracelet and the fake identification card.

While the fake identification card had an accurate depiction of his facial features, his hair and eye color were vastly different. Beside the photo, there were a few personal details listed such as his full name, age, gender, and occupation.

"Ashton Vior, age 18, male, blacksmith's apprentice," he recited.

Then, Lucian tested the appearance-altering bracelet. Clasping the bracelet onto his wrist and looking into the mirror, Lucian saw the person on the identification card staring back. Like in the photo, his smooth, shiny blond hair and blue eyes had been replaced with coarse, dark-brown hair and violet eyes. He shuddered at the very sight.

Lucian looked exactly like *him*...

Due to sheer shock, Lucian felt his knees weaken, so he sat on the side of the bed. Diving deeper into his thoughts, he lingered on whether he truly wanted to concede to Eva's reckless mission or take his chances as a runaway in Terras. His decision came down to one simple factor: If he ran away, what would happen to Seraphina and Titania?

After coming to terms with his mission, Lucian started to mentally and physically prepare himself. First, he clasped the mana-restricting earrings onto his ears. Almost immediately, he felt his mana flow constrict. Next, he fastened the bracelet onto his left wrist. The sight of his new features still greatly bothered him, but it was a discomfort that he could bear. Finally, Lucian changed his clothes, examining his new outfit in the mirror. It consisted of a royal-purple shirt with muddy-brown pants, reflecting Terrasian's distinct style. A perfect disguise, as one would say.

Lying on the floor from the day prior were his old clothes. From his pants, Lucian retrieved the one item worth keeping: Melinda's Credit Slip. He transferred both the Credit Slip and the fake identification card into his pocket.

Now, the only remaining problem was his white cloak. Darius, at the very least, had seen Lucian wearing this piece of clothing. The cloak had become his trademark look. After some deliberation, he decided to leave the cloak along with its contents in his room. If he were ever to be searched, these items would be hard to explain. Instead of a mole infiltrating The Royal Guards, he would easily turn into a trapped bird in an iron cage.

After tidying up his room, Lucian left in search of his guide, Lawrence.

Surprisingly, it took less than a few minutes to find his guide, Lawrence, who was lounging on a window frame at the heart of the house. He was silently reading a book. Even without saying a word, Lawrence reacted to Lucian's approaching footsteps. Meeting eyes with Lawrence was like staring straight at a lion.

"Looks like the sacrificial lamb has come seeking its slaughter," Lawrence wryly said, a lackluster smile forming on his lips. "But I guess even a sacrifice has its use."

"So much for a guide," Lucian mumbled.

Ignoring Lucian's comment, Lawrence started to talk strategy, "Win your first match by a margin using your physical strength enhanced by your mana, defeat your second opponent with basic sorcery, and then win your third and final match using your sword. Got it?"

Fairly surprised by Lawrence's advice, Lucian compliantly nodded in response.

"I have a question."

"Spit it out."

"During her explanation of my mission yesterday, Eva only said that I needed to enter the middle ranks and infiltrate the palace," Lucian stated. "What exactly am I supposed to do once I'm inside?"

A bulging vein appeared on Lawrence's forehead as he exclaimed, "I can't believe that dense woman gave you a mission without explaining anything!"

Lucian looked to the side to avoid starting another fight.

"I'll only say this once, so listen closely," Lawrence

grumbled. "The mist outside of Blackridge isn't mere mist... It's poison."

Lucian remembered the sight of the sickly villagers when he had first arrived.

A cold shiver ran down his spine.

"W-What do you mean by 'poison'?"

Lawrence clasped his hands together and leaned forward while saying, "We believe that the poison comes straight from The Terrasian Palace."

"That doesn't make any sense," Lucian stated. "If that was true, wouldn't the citizens in Blackridge be the most affected?"

"They are, Lucian," Lawrence confirmed. "Outwardly, they cover their symptoms with cosmetic products. Inwardly, they subdue their pain with medicinal drugs."

Lucian remembered their empty, glazed-over eyes.

"Then, those drugs are—"

"—manufactured and distributed by The Terrasian Palace," Lawrence said, finishing Lucian's statement.

"So that's why I need to infiltrate the palace..." Lucian started to link everything together. "Eva wants me to find a way to permanently shut down the manufacturing plant."

"Bingo!"

Scratching his head, Lucian asked, "Are you sure that I'm the right person for the job? I know what Eva said, but..."

"Listen, kid. Once Eva's made up her mind about something, it's almost impossible to change it," Lawrence said, withholding a scowl.

"I know, but you're more fit for this mission than I am," Lucian admitted.

"Of course, I am," Lawrence responded, matter-of-factly. "The tournament's starting soon, so let's head out."

THE TOURNAMENT'S LOCATION WAS A LOT MORE lackluster than Lucian expected. Instead of a grandiose stadium like that of The Battle of the Bronze, it was held in an abandoned section of Blackridge with only flimsy ropes blocking off the surrounding streets. The entire space was an open area with little to no restrictive barriers, making it difficult to know where the arena and participants' line started and ended.

Once Lucian stepped into the participant's line, he noticed that there were way more applicants than he had originally thought. People of all ages, genders, and races were there to fight for entrance into The Royal Guards. Lucian couldn't believe the turnout for this tournament. Since this was a monthly event, he expected only a few applicants, but he surmised that there were at least a hundred in the crowd.

After a long wait, Lucian reached the front of the line. Just like Lawrence explained earlier, the worker who verified the applicants' identities and handed them their admissions ticket had the eyes of a dead fish and a scruffy appearance. It wasn't just the worker, either. When Lucian looked around, he realized that the participants themselves were like toy soldiers marching to the same tune and following orders.

Even weirder, the judges of the tournament couldn't be seen in the crowd. Lucian flashed Lawrence a worried look; however, his guide didn't even flinch at the sight. With a voice like a whisper, Lawrence said, "Keep your emotions subdued, Ashton."

"Even if I show my emotions, it's not like they'll notice," Lucian said, his eyes scanning the sweaty sea of flesh.

"Well, whatever you do, don't draw any unnecessary attention to yourself. If Captain Darius or Vice-Captain Angelique becomes interested in you, you're as good as dead."

Lucian nervously whistled, averting his eyes, thinking, *I wonder if Eva told him that we've already met multiple times.*

Before they could continue their conversation, Lucian

and Lawrence were right in front of the worker. Mechanically, the worker stated, "Identification card, please."

After handing the identification card to the worker, Lucian let out a short breath. Not even one minute later, the worker returned the card and a white button with the number "32" on it. As soon as Lucian clipped the white button onto his shirt, reality finally settled in, and a ball of stress formed in the pit of his stomach.

Within the blink of an eye, the tournament began, and an unseen loudspeaker announced the registered applicants and their opponents. Lucian, disguised as Ashton, had his first match against number "23," a man registered under the nickname, Merciless Mo. Out of all the matches announced, Lucian was the tenth match, so he had some time to spare. Based on the number of applicants, in total, twenty first-round matches would take place.

Under Lawrence's guidance, Lucian decided to carefully watch the prior matches to understand the rules and the techniques used. He was, after all, supposed to blend in with the other applicants by fighting in the traditional Terrasian style. In order to memorize and eventually mimic the style's unique movements, he kept his eyes peeled for each and every offensive and defensive pattern. By the time that it was his turn to fight, Lucian had learned the basics.

Luckily, the previous matches accumulated to at least three hours, which provided him ample time to play multiple scenarios in his head using the newly obtained skills. Although he wasn't aware of it at the time, his learning speed was unnaturally fast. Thanks to his grueling training and life-threatening experiences, he had been bestowed with irreplaceable skills. This tournament, although not intentional, acted to test them.

As a final farewell, Lawrence whispered in his ear, "Don't die."

With those final words, his guide disappeared into the crowd. Lucian, fighting as Ashton, made his way into the center of the fighting ring. Like all of the other matches, he was surrounded by layers and layers of spectators, blocking off any escape routes. The judges' locations were still undisclosed, as they had yet to make an appearance.

His opponent, Merciless Mo, appeared from the opposite direction, wielding what looked like a metal spear with sharp spikes sticking out on all sides. The weapon looked like it hadn't been maintained in many years, as the metal spikes were rusted. Other than that, the man looked like any other brute-force fighter: He had big, protruding muscles and a head devoid of hair other than a gel-formed Mohawk.

So that's why he's called Merciless Mo, Lucian noted.

Remembering what Lawrence had instructed him to do, Lucian fought only with his mana-enforced bare fists. Due to his training with Aaron and then with Leon, his enhanced physical attacks were more than Merciless Mo could handle. Lucian was quick, with or without magic. Although he was supposed to win by a small margin, Lucian's strength overwhelmed his opponent. It only took two to three punches to disable Mo. His fourth and final punch sent the burly man flying into the unwelcoming crowd of spectators.

Lucian worried that his easy win would draw too much suspicion, but the crowd's reaction was mild at best. He slipped back into the crowd of spectators. Both his disguise, which masked his outer features, and the earrings, which restricted his mana flow, were working, so he was able to easily avoid any unnecessary attention.

Following the first round, only twenty applicants remained. Unsurprisingly, the second round went exactly as Lawrence had planned. Lucian attacked with some basic spells and battled back and forth until the opponent ran out of mana. At some point, he actually felt bad for his opponent, who struggled against Lucian's constant attacks.

In the third match, however, Lucian struggled due to a surprise. With only ten applicants left, Lucian expected the third round to follow the same format. So, something was off when all ten applicants were herded into the fighting arena.

Stepping out from the crowd, the hidden judges finally

made their appearance. Darius, Angelique, and one other judge surfaced out of the sea of spectators. They had completely subdued their auras to blend in with the crowd, a truly terrifying skill.

Instead of a one-on-one fight, Darius announced a peculiar, alternative type of match. In an authoritative and resounding voice, he stated, "We are truly grateful for this month's applicants! We, the judges, have decided to make this final match different from anything that we've ever done before. As you can tell, we've assembled our remaining ten applicants in the fighting arena. As for the rules for the final match, it will be a one-versus-ten match with one of us judges battling against all of the ten applicants."

The crowd burst into perfectly synchronized applause, the scene and atmosphere mirroring Angelique's initial appearance during The Battle of the Bronze. Submerging any external sign of discomfort, Lucian remained steady as a rock. Any unnatural expression of anxiety or fear would alert the judges and nullify his cover.

"And since it wouldn't be fun for us to select a representative," Darius proclaimed, "We will allow one of the applicants to choose."

"Now, who," Darius asked, addressing the crowd, "should we give that privilege to?"

"Ashton! Ashton! Ashton!" the crowd chanted.

Darius's eyes roamed over the applicants until they interlocked with Lucian's. "Well, it looks like you're the man of honor today. Who do you choose, Ashton?"

Lucian's mind raced with every experience he had undergone with Darius and Angelique. If anyone could expose his identity in close quarters, it would've been them. His eyes flicked back and forth between them, and then he remembered the other judge's existence. The third judge had a pale-white mask covering his face and a black cloak hiding his figure. Unlike the other two, this judge was less intimidating. Lucian had no other choice than to...

Lifting his finger slowly but surely, he pointed at the unknown judge. "I choose him."

"Looks like we have a match!" Darius proclaimed to the spectators. "I will count down from three, and then the match will start! All ten applicants, please prepare yourselves."

Darius started the countdown.

The rhythm of Lucian's heart hastened.

"Three."

"Two."

"One."

"Let the match begin!"

13

PLAYING THE PART

 *Blackridge*

L ike a flash of lightning, the masked judge wiped half of the applicants out of the arena with a single attack. It happened so fast that they were unable to even react. Whether it was a swing of a sword or sorcery, Lucian didn't know. All he knew was that the remaining five applicants, including himself, would share the same fate if they didn't act fast. It seemed like the other four applicants had the same idea, as they rushed their opponent without hesitation.

The masked judge flicked them away like harmless flies, blocking and dodging their attacks with ease. Even with the other four applicants attacking him at the same time, the judge was unfazed. Watching the first attack, Lucian knew that a reckless attack wouldn't work. Instead, he focused on utilizing his limited mana to prepare a concentrated attack. He evenly divided his mana into his feet for speed and his hands for power. Running around the outer perimeter to increase his speed, he looked for an opening or distraction.

The other four applicants were perfectly in sync, like puppets. Almost like a choreographed performance, the four applicants and the judge swapped back and forth from attack to defense. Unlike normal fights, everything was too planned.

Lucian, however, was too focused on creating a chance. He regulated his breath and his heartbeat, concealing his presence and letting the other four draw the most attention. He lessened his mana distribution, creating a steady stream. The moment that the four applicants slightly disturbed the judge's footing, Lucian attacked. He used his legs to propel himself upward and forward.

Midair, he drew his fist back, swinging during the downward acceleration of his jump. Bringing the full force of a mana-infused punch, Lucian made an impact with the judge's face, hurling him to the ground and making him roll like a barrel several feet backward. With a rush of adrenaline, a spark of satisfaction spread across Lucian's face.

"Don't let this chance go to waste!" one of the four applicants commanded. "Everyone, attack!"

Unlike the last synchronized attack, two of the applicants stayed in the back, reciting an incantation beneath their breath. Rays of light shot from their hands, hitting the judge before he could fully recover from the previous attack.

The spell's success signaled the other two applicants to attack. They sprinted toward the judge, smashing their fists into the ground on both sides of him. At first, it looked like a failed attempt, but in less than a second, the ground roared open, a giant chasm forming underneath him. As swift as the first attack, the masked judge evaded the pitfall, easily passing by his attackers. After knocking down the two closest applicants, he raced toward the two Sorcerers. Before Lucian could warn them, the masked judge had incapacitated them.

Now, Lucian was the only one left standing after the blitz attack from his opponent. Even though his allies fought well, they were still like puppets on a string. They were no match for the masked man.

"Ignis, this is a good time to wake up, you lazy sword!" Lucian demanded.

"It's not my fault that you don't appreciate my existence," Ignis pouted. "I've waited a week for you to realize that I was giving you the cold shoulder."

What a passive-aggressive sword, Lucian thought, rolling his eyes. *Okay, my wonderful partner who does no wrong, will you help me not to die!?*

The masked judge now turned his attention to Lucian, crossing the distance between them in seconds. Lucian unsheathed Ignis as fast as he could, only having time to barely block the first attack with his blade. The mere impact of the judge's fist on the blade made Lucian fly backward. While Lucian was certain of his physical strength, his opponent was like a monster. Even so, a part of Lucian felt almost excited in the moment—like his body was craving a powerful adversary. He subconsciously cracked a smile.

"Looks like I chose the right judge, after all," Lucian exclaimed, a glint of glee reflecting in his eyes. "Come at me!"

Lucian blocked the barrage of punches while managing to swing his sword at the judge. If he could maintain enough mana in his feet to dodge, he would be able to evade anything fatal. The masked judge, however, seemed like a machine, simply executing the same attack and defense patterns. After a while, Lucian became accustomed to the judge's fighting style, allowing Lucian to further pressure his opponent with several direct hits and force him on the defensive.

Something strange caught Lucian's eye while

exchanging blows. Like Lucian, Ignis had also undergone a drastic change in his appearance. Now, Ignis appeared as a standard sword with no fancy embellishments and a muted gray handle. This minor detail was enough to draw his attention away from his opponent for a split second.

In that instance, the masked judge flung him to the ground. After being smashed down to the dirt, Lucian received countless kicks to the gut, causing him to cough up saliva and blood. In response, he poured his mana into his feet, positioned himself to face his opponent, and produced a powerful kick that knocked out his opponent's knees.

Although the attack awarded him a few seconds, Lucian returned to a standing position, gripping Ignis's handle even tighter than before. Sweat streamed down his face and his body like a fierce rainstorm. Subconsciously, he tried to draw on Ignis's powers to a dangerous level. At his current mana level, he wouldn't survive if he continued to use Ignis. The feeling of exhilaration seized Lucian, however, making him forget his surroundings and original purpose.

"Anymore, and you'll lose consciousness!" Ignis piped up. "Don't forget your purpose and who you are! My wielder right now isn't Lucian Roux... It's Ashton Vior!"

Ashton Vior. Yes, I am Ashton Vior.

Subduing his overflowing emotions, Lucian decided to

sheathe Ignis and pursue hand-to-hand combat with what little mana he had left. Laughter escaped his lips, riling up both the judges and the spectators. The masked judge showed a split second of hesitation before continuing to fight. But none of that mattered to Lucian.

All he could feel was his internal mana pool draining to a scarily low level. For conservation purposes, he released the mana in his feet, focusing what little was left that he had into his palms. A strange, one-chance strategy formulated in his head, as he braced for his opponent's fists to make an impact on his stomach.

The moment that the masked judge's fists slammed into his stomach, he absorbed the full force while abandoning any sort of defense. The pain kept his body alert, as the accumulating mana in his palms reached a peak. The masked judge stalled in place, thinking that he had won.

Lucian took advantage of his moment of hesitation, pushing the masked judge's chest with his mana-infused palms. Even without physical power behind the push, the judge shot backward, crashing to the arena floor, even further than Lucian's punch had thrown him earlier.

Amazingly, Lucian scored a huge advantage. However, instead of pursuing the fallen judge to finish the fight, his eyes were stuck on his palms. The moment that he pushed the judge's chest, he felt something...soft. Softer than what a trained male soldier's chest should've felt like. His head tried to wrap around what he thought he had felt, but his mind was distracted by the constant yells of the crowd to finish the job. Even so, his feet were firmly planted in place.

He was about to say something when Darius's voice resounded over the speaker and announced, "Ashton Vior has successfully defeated our representative! Congratulations on his successes in battle. Following the treatment of any injuries sustained in the final match, we will announce the results of the tournament."

Lucian knew that he shouldn't have won that match. Not only was the judge going easy on him, but he was also supposed to fight as Ashton Vior, not Lucian Roux. By the time that Darius announced the end of the match, the masked judge had disappeared from the spot where he had collapsed. Lucian's exchange with the judge was peculiar and strange, and he knew he never wanted to fight with that guy again...if it was a guy at all.

AFTER THE PARTICIPANTS' WOUNDS HAD BEEN treated, all of them lined up in the arena. Darius and Angelique approached them, holding official certificates and metal pins.

"Congratulations to our brave contestants!" Darius declared. "Starting with the bronze awards, Applicant Number 18 displayed superior physical prowess, thus earning a bronze pin and acceptance into the bottom ranks of The Royal Guards. Likewise, Applicant Number 2 and Applicant Number 36 displayed an equal mastery in sorcery, thus earning a bronze pin and acceptance into the bottom ranks of The Royal Guards as well. Next, for the silver awards, Applicant Number 29 expressed impressive physical power and exceptional leadership capabilities, thus earning a silver pin and acceptance into the middle ranks of The Royal Guards. Congratulations to you four applicants for displaying a good fight."

Lucian, who stood as still as a statue, started to fidget when his name wasn't mentioned alongside the other four applicants. He wondered if he had been disqualified by a technicality.

"As everyone knows, there was only one applicant who managed to stay conscious during the entire match and delivered a critical hit against a judge," Darius explained. "Applicant Number 32, you are a one-in-a-million talent. I have high hopes for your future, and I intend to see to it myself. Although very rare, Applicant Number 32 is awarded a golden pin and earned acceptance into the top ranks of The Royal Guards! Everyone, please show your support for the official eleventh member of The Royal Guards."

Lucian's mind went blank.

Even when he was handed the metal pin and the plastic card, he couldn't compute what just happened. Getting into the bottom ranks would've been merciful compared to this travesty. He was practically being thrown into a pit of vipers, all waiting to strike at him. He was so out of sorts that he didn't even notice when Darius came to greet him.

"Forgive my rotten memory, but for the record, what should I call you?" Darius asked, grinning ear to ear. "You're going to be a close comrade of mine, so I thought we should get to know each other well."

"A-Ashton Vior," he blurted out, hastily saying anything that came to mind. "A-And that's not necessary. I wouldn't want to be a burden…"

"Well, with your skills, I can assure you that you're anything but a burden, young man." Darius chuckled, slapping Lucian's back playfully. "To be more serious, I am proud to admit you into the highest ranks of The Terrasian Army. Welcome to The Royal Guards, Ashton Vior."

14

A DEN OF LIONS, A GUISE OF LIES

 *Blackridge*

On the outskirts of Blackridge sat the stronghold of The Royal Guards. A massive gray and black stone fortress towered over him. Height-wise, it stood twice as tall as The Holy Chapel in Caelum. Widthwise, it covered the area of several districts combined. On the perimeter, Lucian spotted circular lookout towers, fixed artillery on the fortress walls, and an imposing metal portcullis protecting the entrance.

"Hurry up, kid," Angelique said, flatly. "Otherwise, we'll miss dinner."

Ushered into the fortress's gatehouse, Lucian followed Darius and Angelique closely. Contrary to his expectations, the courtyard was surprisingly silent. He had imagined groups of soldiers training and performing combat drills, but there was no such sight. Instead, everything from the fixed artillery to the lookout towers appeared abandoned, eerily so.

Crossing through the deserted courtyard, Lucian couldn't contain his curiosity and started to lag behind his superiors as he searched for some sign of life. Once he noticed how far he was behind them, he jogged to catch up.

"Excuse me, Captain Darius?" he inquired, slightly out of breath. "Where *is* everyone?"

Darius lessened his pace and responded, "Aside from a few cooks and maids, we're the only ones here, Ashton. The other eight members are either out patrolling their assigned regions in Terras or on foreign expeditions."

"Enough chit-chatting, you two," Angelique interjected. "If you delay my dinner with your insignificant gibberish, then I'll feed you both to the dragons."

The hairs on the back of Lucian's neck prickled at the mention of dragons.

"D-Dragons?" he asked, sweat forming on his forehead. "Aren't they from old folk tales? Like the ones you tell children to scare them at night?"

"Not quite," Darius replied. "But you'll see in time.

There's no need to rush anything. Also, cool it with the fear tactics, Angelique."

She clicked her tongue in annoyance. "Fine, but if he gets in my way, I swear I'll make him into dragon fodder."

Picking up her pace, she flew past them, heading through a set of double wooden doors.

Darius rested his hand reassuringly on Lucian's shoulder and said, "Don't worry about her, Ashton. She's the type to get her feathers easily ruffled...and you did defeat someone that she lost to in the past."

"Ah, that masked judge," he stated. "Are they also a member of The Royal Guards?"

"Mhm, you could say that." Darius nodded his head. "They don't come by the barracks that often, but once they do, you'll be in for a big surprise."

After a few minutes of walking, they arrived at their destination—a giant building with steel doors. Darius easily pushed the heavy-looking double doors open with one fell swoop. What burst out of the building were wafts of delicious smells and streams of bright lights shooting from hanging crystals. They arrived at the one place where people could just be people, and where one could forget about one's worries in exchange for comfort: the dining hall.

Entering after Darius, Lucian walked over to where Angelique was already perched. She seemed the happiest she had ever been, munching on a juicy-looking meat stick with butter slathered all over it. Lucian's stomach started to growl. He hastily followed Darius to the counter near the kitchen, where the food had been laid out in large trays. Lucian shoveled meat stacks onto a shiny silver plate and poured a dark crimson liquid into his cup. It smelled sweet.

"Going for the good stuff, aren't ya, Ashton?" Darius said, grinning from ear to ear.

Shrugging off the comment, Lucian took his plate and cup back to where Angelique sat. He placed his food and sat in a space or two across from her so that he wouldn't set her off. Goodness knows she had a terrible temper. He quietly ate and drank, listening to Darius drone on about his ventures across Gaia with Angelique's frequent but short sarcastic comments sprinkled into the stories.

After what seemed like a long period of time, Lucian's vision started to blur, and his speech started to slur rather pathetically. "W-what is this drrrrink called?"

"That's dragon's blood," Angelique said with a low, serious tone. "I wouldn't drink anymore if I were you, especially since you *obviously* lack the tolerance for it."

Lucian spat up the liquid he had been sloshing in his mouth, hoarsely coughing it out. Darius slapped his back for support while explaining, "Don't take her too seriously, boy. It's a special type of wine called 'Dragon's Blood.' It's not actually from a dragon."

Darius pointed at the kitchen area and said, "Sorry, kid, I didn't know this was your first time drinking wine. There's a water dispenser in the kitchen you can wash it down with."

Lucian hiccuped, and then he replied, "Got it, boss."

Lucian stood up quickly...maybe too quickly. The blood shot to his head, and he almost threw up on the table. He submerged his feelings of nausea, desperately trying to stop his meal from slithering its way back up. Every step toward the kitchen was a mortifying experience: His balance was off, and his vision blurred so badly that he bumped into several benches and tables, knocking over a few glass plates and goblets. Although Darius assured him everything was alright, Lucian tried to clean up the mess as best as he could.

I'm so embarrassed, he thought. *I'm acting like him, now...*

He eventually made his way to the kitchen entrance, but not without immense humiliation. Reaching the door, he hastily pushed it open, hoping that the worst of his problems was over. Unfortunately for him, however, his drunken state would be the least of his concerns.

Upon entering the kitchen, he stumbled toward the water dispenser. He fumbled to twist the metal faucet open. After a few failed attempts, he finally turned it on, a stream of sparkling water splashing out. He first gulped down as much water as he could. After the water filled the basin beneath the dispenser, he submerged his head in it, the cool water shocking him awake and clearing his senses.

Resurfacing from the water, a pair of brown eyes greeted him from the side of the basin. It took him several seconds to react, but when his mind processed it properly, he fell backward flat on his bottom with a loud *thump!*

Darius called from the dining hall, shouting, "Everything alright in there, Ashton?"

Trying to sound sober, he replied with a simple, "Yes."

What piqued his curiosity more was the owner of the eyes that startled him. Upon closer inspection, he realized that the pair of eyes belonged to a small-statured, dark-haired girl with oh-so-familiar bark-colored irises. Her frame was slim, her cheeks dirty, her hair greasy, and her gown stained and tattered at the hem. Lucian's head tilted to the side, the thought of the girl being a figment of his imagination briefly crossing his mind. After what seemed like a long time staring at her in a daze, the girl approached him slowly, bending down to meet him at eye level.

"Are you a ghost?" Lucian laughed while asking. "Because I may have had a little too much to drink." He clamped his mouth shut, unsure of the way that he sounded. The water started to clear his conscience, and a flood of guilt washed over him.

She sat on her knees, exhibiting through her expression a strange mixture of hope, desperation, and fear. She mouthed many words, none of which Lucian could easily decipher with his nonexistent lip-reading skills. She grew frustrated with his lack of reaction, shaking her head and furrowing her brow. The girl yanked his hand to hers, flipping it over, and using the base of his palm. Her hands and the index finger, which she used to trace the words, were calloused and rough, rubbing against his own.

Looking desperate, she conveyed the start of her message: "Don't trust Da–"

Before she could finish her statement, Darius barged into the kitchen, catching Lucian and the girl clasping hands together like a pair of long-lost lovers. Lucian tried to explain, but he fumbled his words. Darius winked at him and flashed a big, bear-like smile.

"Don't worry, Ashton!" The man roared with amusement. After getting most of his laughter out of his system, Darius stated in a more serious tone, "I understand youthful passions. I too was quite the ladies' man when I was your age. However, how should I say this nicely...? I wouldn't want you to get involved with someone like her. We caught this *rat* in the palace gutters...and let's just say that she paid back her dues."

Darius tapped on his throat three times, where his Adam's apple bulged out.

"I'm not sure I'm following," Lucian said, eyes enlarging. "What do you mean, so she can't...?"

Darius approached the girl, bending down to her eye level and saying, "Show us your sins, child."

The girl's face contorted with fear as she opened her mouth to reveal emptiness...What should've been there wasn't there... Moving from confusion to horror, Lucian completely snapped out of his drunken daze.

A minute or so passed before Lucian could even look at Darius. When they locked eyes, Darius stated, "It's been a long day. Let's get you to your new home away from home."

Lifted by his upper arm, Darius dragged Lucian out of the kitchen. The image of the girl plagued him, as he couldn't bear the thought of how the atrocity occurred. Lucian finally realized why Evangeline chose to send Lucian, not Lawrence, on this mission.

Breaking Lucian out of his thoughts, Darius proclaimed, "Here we are!"

Lightly pushing him into an uninhabited room, Lucian looked around at his new "home." The room was just like the others that he had stayed in during his travels. Aside from the branded logo of The Royal Guards' insignia on the curtains, bedspread, and towels, Lucian would've thought he was at any other inn or guild.

"Ahem," Darius coughed. "Apologies for any wear and

tear, this fortress hasn't seen any significant renovations since ten...no, twenty years?"

"It won't be an issue," Lucian responded. "I'm used to some dirt and dust."

Darius smiled reassuringly. "Well, then, I should let you get a good night's rest. We have an early morning tomorrow for your first patrol, so you need to be well rested."

"Thank you," Lucian responded.

Darius left him alone in the room. He plopped onto the bed, blankly staring at the ceiling. The images of his father and the girl continued to flash in his mind, making it impossible for him to sleep peacefully. *I'm so stupid*, he thought. *Stop letting your guard down!*

He initially imagined a brave rescue scenario where, under the original plan, as a middle-ranked soldier, he would infiltrate the depths of the palace's underground prison cells. After locating Lorin, he would destroy the manufacturing plant and then whisk her away to the safety of the ATF headquarters. However, another issue arose after these delusions faded. While the prison break would've been difficult, this scenario was no piece of cake either. Now, he was under direct surveillance by The Captain of The Royal Guards himself, the biggest obstacle to his mission.

After several hours of rumination, he heard a knock on

the door. It was so quiet he thought his mind was playing tricks on him; however, he knew by now that it was better to be cautious than to be caught off guard, especially in the dead of night. Thanks to someone...

Tiptoeing toward the door, he placed his ear against it, trying to audibly discern if someone was still there. He lay flat on his belly, peeking under the door's narrow opening, visually confirming that whoever knocked had vanished.

He did, however, become suspicious when he saw an envelope poking out between the floorboards right in front of his room. Curious enough to take the risk, he slipped his fingers under the opening and pinched the parchment between his index and middle fingers, carefully sliding it into his room.

He crawled toward the window, where the moon rays trickled inside. Tearing open the edge of the envelope, he realized there were two pages neatly folded inside. He unfolded both but first focused on a shoddily drawn sketch. After turning it sideways, he realized it was the missing section of the palace that Lorin had been tasked to complete.

The second paper was an encrypted letter.

"You're not alone. While the rat has been trapped, the bird is still flying its course. Follow the guidance given under the stars. Remember the Fallen, for they will rise again."

Just like the haunting warnings in his recurring nightmares, the ominous text on the walls in Caelum, and the damning prophecies of the ancient gods, these words pierced him sharper than any knife could have.

In the darkness of the room with the shadows as his only companions, he whispered the last sentence under his breath, "Remember the Fallen, for they will rise again."

15

A DANCE TO THE DEATH

Tottering back and forth and swaying left and right, Lucian tried matching his dance partner's movements. One step after another, he kept tripping over his own feet. With each minute that passed, Lucian grew more and more frustrated. Moving along with the music was an impossible feat for him, as he was always a spectator—never a participant—of the traditional dances in Caelum.

Angelique, at first, patiently led him through the steps. However, after the fourth or fifth time stomping on her feet, the creases on her forehead grew scarily sharp. "Darius, I can't teach someone with two left feet how to dance," she complained. "It'd be easier to just manipulate his mana and treat him like a puppet on a string."

Darius, who had been keenly watching from the shady side of the courtyard, approached them. Per usual, a big grin flashed on his face as he said, "You know that's not allowed, Angel. The Founder's Festival is right around the corner."

"When you told me I needed to train, I thought you meant *actual* training," Lucian whined. "I didn't know dancing was a vital duty of The Royal Guards."

Scratching the back of his head, Darius replied, "Well, not usually, but I'll let you in on a little secret. On the final day of The Founder's Festival, The Terrasian Royal Palace is set to hold a grand ball. Since the palace gates remain open during this time and many nobles and royals are in attendance, security needs to be even tighter than usual. We, the highest order of The Royal Guards, will attend the ball to protect the emperor from any threats inside the ballroom."

"Wait, but don't guards normally stand on the sidelines?" Lucian questioned. "There's no reason for us to be dancing alongside the guests, right?"

"I agree," Angelique stated.

"It's a direct order from the emperor," Darius answered. "Think of it like a vacation. Angel needs it more than anyone. She's fifteen, but she already has more wrinkles than I do!"

Baring her teeth at Darius like a wild animal, she swung at him. After a failed swipe, she said, "I can fix your forehead if that's the issue."

"F-Fifteen?" Lucian let out a gasp. "But you look like you're only twelve years old. Did you refuse to eat your vegetables and drink your milk?"

"You're dead meat too, Ashton!" she said, swinging her other arm at him.

Lucian jumped swiftly backward out of harm's way. Painfully aware of what would happen if she landed a swing on him, he maintained a good gap between them.

Darius clapped his hands together while saying, "Let's take a break, shall we? Angelique, go check and see if our outfits for the festival have arrived. As for Ashton, I'll show you around the fortification more extensively today, since we didn't get a chance yesterday."

Lucian's eyes lit up, wondering what Darius wanted to show him.

The first stop was the armory, where all types of weapons were stored. Unlike Barren's shop, the armory contained everything from crossbows to axes. The second stop was the lookout points atop the walls surrounding the perimeter of the fortress. The towers were so tall that both Darius and

Lucian were slightly winded by the time they reached the top. From the first lookout point, Lucian could see a broader view of The Terras Empire, everything from the palace to the outskirts of Blackridge where they originally entered.

Turning to his left, Lucian saw several spirals of strange black fumes seeping out of The Terrasian Palace. Squinting his eyes, Lucian noticed the source of the fumes seemed to originate from the base of the building, working its way up to the top. Lucian double-checked to ensure that he wasn't imagining the fumes. At the same time, he confirmed that Darius chose to ignore them. To not draw unnecessary attention to himself, Lucian pretended to be marveling at the palace's architecture.

After analyzing the landscape, Lucian and Darius made their third and final stop at the training grounds. Unlike the courtyard with its defined barriers, the training grounds existed outside of the courtyard. If there was a word to best define the training grounds, it would be *unrefined*. A mixture of dirt and weeds made up the base, and the visible markings on the ground delineating the archery range from the battle zone were blurred from lack of maintenance.

What was even more concerning, however, was the look of despair on Darius's face, as he stared off into space. "I'm sorry, Ashton, the training grounds haven't been used in quite some time. You're probably already aware of this by now, but the upper echelon of The Royal Guards isn't here often enough to put this place to good use."

Walking over to a rotting wooden bench on the eastern side of the training grounds, Darius sat down. Lucian followed suit, sitting beside his superior and waiting for Darius to continue his story. An awkward silence ensued. The wind whirled around them, picking up dust from the ground.

Firmly grabbing his right knee, Darius said, "Before the new emperor seized the throne, The Terras Empire was a very different place. Ya'know, the previous emperor wasn't really a tyrant. He had an iron fist when it came to following the rules, but he wasn't abusing his power. We had a lot more soldiers enlisting in The Terrasian Army back then. Even though they knew the days of war were over, they still burned bright with determination to protect these lands."

"What happened to them?" Lucian asked.

"When the new emperor took the throne, they were whisked away from the fortress. Whether to destabilize another nation or to manufacture weapons of war, they became mere tools for a new regime. Many died from over-work or enemy warriors uncovering their true identities. Even the young warriors whom I trained during my days as an instructor never returned home," he said, a sourness to his tone. "If only..."

"If only...what?"

"No, never mind me, I'm just an old cog in a busted machine."

"Those soldiers were lucky to have you, regardless."

"Ah, I spoke too much about myself," Darius said, his words trailing off. "You didn't join The Royal Guards for chit chat, did you?"

"Things change, Captain Darius," Lucian said. "Nothing ever remains the same. That's an inevitable part of life. Besides, evil can't reign forever."

"Is that why you're here, Ashton?"

"Hmm? Oh, no, I don't dream of doing anything revolutionary," Lucian said. "There's only one thing I've ever wanted out of life."

"What's that?"

Freedom.

"To be stronger," Lucian lied. "I'd like to be the strongest warrior there ever was. When I fight, I want to win, no matter what."

"That's a very admirable goal, Ashton," Darius said. "I'll support you, as I too once shared your dream."

Breaching the topic that had been circling in his mind, Lucian inquired, "I'm curious about that *rat* I met the other day... What was her name again?"

"Lorin," Darius answered.

"Right, Lorin. I was wondering what she did to have her t-tongue removed."

"Well, let's just say that rats have a way of stealing things that don't belong to them. Whether that be information or belongings, rats are as bold as they are vile."

"What did she steal?"

"She stole a copy of the palace's blueprints. You can only imagine what our enemies would do if they had something as crucial as that. We can't allow them to attack us again. I'll never allow it. And with The Founder's Festival coming up, we have to be on our guard."

"Do you know what'll happen to the rat?"

Darius slapped him on the back reassuringly while saying, "You're a compassionate fellow, aren't you? Maybe too nice, for that matter. She'll be treated like the rats before her. After we've extracted the necessary information from her, she'll be exterminated."

"E-Exterminated? What do you mean? And how do you extract that information from her without her, well, her tongue?"

Darius copied the motion that he performed the other day, but this time, his fingers tapped the side of his cranium rather than his Adam's apple. "There are more ways than one to extract information. Words can be tricky, so we like to deal with memories and thoughts instead."

"Y-You can read her thoughts?" Lucian asked, hesitantly.

"Not me," Darius stated. "Do you remember The Royal Guard you fought the other day? The masked one with an unreadable temper? That was Lieutenant Rosalie, an excellent fighter, mind reader, and war strategist. She's out on active duty today near the border, but she should return in time for the festival."

"D-Did you just say, 'Rosalie'?" Lucian asked, his voice slightly shaking. "Where's she from?"

"I doubt you've ever met her, as she's more of the silent and prickly type, but I guess I can throw you a bone," Darius said. "Her name is Rosalie Roux. She's originally from a small village in the southwest called Caelum."

"Caelum? I've never heard of that village before," Lucian lied. "What kind of place is it, if I may ask?"

"I don't know too much about the area either. All I've heard is that it was an isolated village in the middle of The Sage's Forest."

"What do you mean, it *was*?"

"Because, according to Rosalie, it's been completely destroyed."

"Destroyed!" Lucian's voice went up an octave. "What happened?"

"You're fairly interested in a place that no longer exists. I suppose the younger you are, the more curious you can be," Darius said. "You see, Rosalie isn't the chatty type, but I was able to get *some* explanation out of her. Even with the combined strength of the Elders and the Reincarnates, it wasn't enough to ward *them* off."

"*Them?*" Lucian asked, frantically.

"You see, a pack of enraged monsters breached the barrier and attacked the village."

Panic consumed Lucian, and he desperately asked, "What happened to the villagers? Did anyone survive? Monsters shouldn't have been able to break the barrier."

"That's the thing, Ashton," Darius explained. "The monsters didn't break the barrier...a human did...and then mass slaughter ensued. Rosalie said she was the only survivor, poor thing."

"Who would do such a thing?"

"The same person who killed that poor boy," Darius said, sighing. "Rosalie said the attacker was an *outsider*."

Lucian keeled over, burying his face in his hands. His breathing quickened, and his head started pounding. Flashes of images entered his head at such a fast pace that he couldn't properly process them. The images merged, forming a single, coherent memory.

The memory began with a wide shot of Aaron and Lucian splitting up in Master Felix's observatory after the failed Succession Ceremony. After Aaron pushed Lucian into the secret tunnel, the memory continued, but not from Lucian's perspective. The scenery suddenly shifted once again to The Sage's Forest. A cloaked figure stood before the barrier.

Taking off his hood, the figure was revealed to be Aaron. He took out his sword, Phantom, which was the very sword that had been confiscated in Caelum. Lucian watched in horror as Aaron drove the tip of his blade into the barrier. The barrier let out its last cry, its screams sounding like the shattering of glass. As the barrier broke, Lucian yelled out to him, but no matter how loud he screamed and cursed, his words didn't reach Aaron.

Before Lucian could fully see the scene where the monsters attacked the village, he returned to the training grounds. He felt extremely lightheaded, and his body dropped to the ground. Before losing consciousness, Lucian saw Darius coming to his aid with a worried face. Although Darius's lips were moving, Lucian couldn't understand anything.

With his final fragment of consciousness, Lucian lamented, *Ah, it's you again, Aaron. Why is it always you?*

16

THE FOUNDER'S FESTIVAL

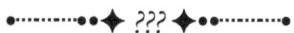

Far above the clouds, another realm existed—one of peace. Like a bird, Lucian soared in the skies, flying toward an endless expanse of floating islands. The wind caressed his cheeks, while the sun rays warmed his soul. He felt free.

This freedom, unfortunately, wasn't meant to last forever. The foreboding voice that followed him no matter where he went called out to him, "*YOU MUST CHOOSE.*"

This time, however, it wasn't speaking to him but rather someone else in the distance. Following the voice, he landed hesitantly on one of the islands. The ground beneath him was filled with lush green grass and blooming multicolored buds. With every step, his feet felt like they were gliding forward. If he wasn't careful, he might float off again, never reaching the place where he needed to be.

Continuing to move forward for what felt like ages, Lucian reached a place where the voice was clearest. Grand ivory pillars pierced through the sky, reaching all the way from the world above to the lowest depths of the world below. Widthwise, they were as large as a kingdom, stretching out farther than the eye could see. He marveled at how the sunlight reflected off their smooth surfaces.

Standing near one of The Heavenly Pillars, an ephemeral figure lingered. His skin emitted a golden glow, and his crimson-red hair flowed in the wind like dancing flames. He seemed to be speaking to someone as he rested his hand on the side of the pillar. Drawn to this mysterious figure, Lucian walked toward him without a worry in the world.

Getting close enough to almost touch him, Lucian asked, "What are you doing here? What is this place?"

The figure didn't seem to hear him. The man's eyes were wholly fixated on the pillar alone, as he let out the words, "I choose the realm governed by Gaia, The Earthly Realm. That is my final decision."

The same foreboding voice demanding the choice replied, "Are you sure? This choice will only lead to ruin for all the realms. Are you willing to bear the eternal curse and damnation? Are they—these humans—worth your concern?"

Yelling out into the void of space, the figure proclaimed, "I have made my choice, High Judge of The Heavenly Realms! I won't allow •••• to triumph! Even if I fall, I shall save my comrades, and they will rise once more."

"Truly, I am The High Judge of The Heavenly Realm," the voice declared. "I shall respect your choice, but heed my warning, O god of destruction. By destroying The Heavenly Pillars, you shall be hated by god and by man alike. Your days shall be filled with pain worse than death, and your soul shall wither away like a flower in the blizzard of winter. Never forget the sin that you have committed today, for you shall never find peace while your enemy lives."

The god of destruction bowed deeply with his knees planted on the grass. With only a few words, he replied, "I shall do so, O great judge of the gods. I shall always remember the Fallen, for they will rise again."

"May the fate of the realms guide you in your journey, Morpheus, god of destruction and brother of Adonis."

Lucian's jaw dropped open while watching the scene unfold before him. Before he could say a word, another figure appeared out of thin air: Adonis. Like in the vision back at Maverick's store, the twin gods started bickering, and then they progressed into all-out fighting.

While Lucian was watching, a wave of rage swelled inside him. After a few minutes, Lucian's emotions flooded out from deep within him: a raging river turning into a colossal tsunami surging with anger and hatred.

He openly cried out, screaming the words, "Curse you, Morpheus! Why did you have to drag me into your mess? Why couldn't you reincarnate as someone else's child? Why did you choose me? Why, me!?"

Of the twin gods, Morpheus was the only one who perceived Lucian's presence. Stopping in his tracks, the god of destruction looked at Lucian with a strangely warm expression. As if they were the only two people in the world, Morpheus said to him, "Never forget, my poor Reincarnate, you aren't alone. Seek out the true strength that lies within you. Don't stray from your path and become deceived by people or things of old."

"That's a load of crap! I'm sick of all these riddles, rhymes, and prophecies! Just tell me the truth!"

Fending off his brother's fist, Morpheus said these final words to Lucian, "My dearest Reincarnate, keep these words inscribed in your heart and soul... *Remember the Fallen, for they will rise again.* They shall serve as your guide."

The ground disintegrated beneath him and the twin gods. While the twin gods flew upward and continued to fight, Lucian lost his ability to soar in the skies. He fell to the depths of The Heavenly Realm, reentering the highest reaches of The Earthly Realm. As Lucian fell, Morpheus's words came to mind. But Lucian was lost in Morpheus's final message.

Falling and falling, his eyes grew heavy...

•··········••◆ *Blackridge* ◆••··········•

A FAMILIAR FEELING OF BLANKETS COVERING HIS body was a sign that he had returned. Opening his eyes, a tired-looking Darius sat beside him in a wooden chair too small for his burly build. Lucian chuckled at the ridiculous sight, as Darius's right thigh covered almost the entire seat.

"It's nice to know you can still laugh after all that sleeping," Darius said, standing up from the chair and stretching out his arms. "I thought you were a goner for sure."

Lucian lifted himself off the bed, asking, "How long was I out for? I had the worst nightmare."

"Two full days and nights, Ashton," Darius explained. "Angel's asleep right now, but she's been up day and night caring for you with her healing magic. Thank her when she wakes up. She really put in the hours for you."

"I-I didn't know..."

Two whole days!? I was out for two days and nights! The Founder's Festival must've already started, and I still haven't figured out how to infiltrate the palace, destroy the manufacturing plant, and save Lorin!

"Don't worry about it, kid. We're just glad you're safe," Darius said, reassuringly. "I'll let you bathe and change your clothes. There should be a new pair of clothes waiting for you at the bathhouse. It's near the training grounds on the west side. Once you're done, meet me back in the courtyard. We still have to make the rounds."

"Has The Founder's Festival already started?" Lucian asked, a frown forming on his face.

"Aha!" Darius exclaimed. "Don't look so downtrodden, Ashton! That's exactly where we're headed once you're all set. Even though The Founder's Festival is in full swing, there are still a few days left until the ball, so don't worry! I'll show you the best that The Terras Empire has to offer. I'll even cover your food and drink for today!"

How generous of him. Lucian almost fell for an obvious trap. *No, Lucian, snap out of it! You can't trust him... Not after what Lorin said.*

Nodding his head, Lucian spent the next hour preparing himself. To the bathhouse and back, he felt more refreshed than ever. The new clothes that he changed into were also fluffy and light. They fit him perfectly—almost too perfectly. Tying the white cloak around his neck, he headed out to the courtyard where Darius was waiting for him.

"You ready?" Darius asked.

"Ready as I'll ever be."

After an hour's trek to the center of Blackridge, where the festivities were being held, the venue came into sight. Twinkling crystals illuminated the rows and rows of stalls lining the streets with food, games, and more. Like a little child, Lucian couldn't contain his excitement. Although they were on assignment, the next thirty minutes were anything but work. From delicious meat skewers to sweet lemon drops, Lucian's stomach expanded like a balloon.

Taking a short break from the food, Darius and Lucian tested their strength at an arm-wrestling tournament. Darius won by a landslide, but Lucian performed well enough to land himself in second place. A sense of camaraderie was steadily building between them—something he never would've imagined in his wildest dreams. The leader of the enemy organization and the prophetic child playing such trivial games together seemed unfathomable.

Once the light in the sky vanished, the two of them went to watch the fireworks. A myriad of colors filled the sky, shimmering vibrantly above them. Lucian breathed in the beauty of it all, relaxing his tense muscles.

"Hey, Ashton, I wanted to talk to you about something. Can you lend me your ear?"

"Of course, Captain Darius. I'm all ears."

"Well, we've started to build a rapport, so I just wanted to set the record straight."

"Huh?"

"Those earrings of yours," Darius's voice deepened, "are sorely familiar to me."

Lucian reflexively reached for his ears, ascertaining that the earrings were snuggly clasped in place. In order to divert the conversation and downplay the situation, he said, "Oh, these? I've had them for years, so I don't even remember where I bought them."

"You don't understand what I'm saying," Darius warned. "I know who you really are, and you're not Ashton Vior."

"W-What do you mean?"

"You can't fool me, Lucian Roux," Darius said. "Don't worry, though. I don't plan on exposing you."

"W-What do you mean? Why not?"

"Loyalty, bravery, camaraderie. These are the traits that you've displayed every time that I've seen you," Darius said with a conflicted expression. "You remind me of what The Terrasian Royal Guards once represented a long time ago. I can't let a light like you die out due to the deceit of others. I won't, no, I can't report you."

"You're my enemy, so why?" Lucian asked.

"I've made a lot of mistakes that I'm not proud of. Mistakes that cost the lives of my soldiers and the freedom of my people. I don't want to make the same mistake twice."

"Darius, I don't know what to say..."

"You needn't say anything. Besides, you're not the rat that I was trying to catch anyway."

"But Lorin's been caught already, hasn't she?"

"Not Lorin," Darius said, determination reflecting in his eyes. "You'll see what I mean very soon."

Mixed in with the loud *boom!* and *bang!* of the fireworks, another noise resounded, growing louder and louder with time. Among the joyful giggles, bloodcurdling screams from multiple directions in the venue emerged. Darius and Lucian raced toward the area where the commotion was the loudest. There, Lucian saw something horrifying. What had once been a merry scene of joyous celebration was now a street littered with confetti and corpses.

"W-What in the world?"

Darius rested his right hand on Lucian's shoulder and said to him, in a voice as soft as a whisper, "I'll let you in on the little secret. Look at this disaster and guess the culprit."

"I-I don't know."

As the chorus of cries intensified, the wind carried its wretched tune.

"What if I told you that your beloved ATF caused these casualties? What if I told you that they've been lying to you? About your fate, your future, and your friends?"

"I won't lie and say I've never had any suspicions about ATF," Lucian said, sourly. "But how can I trust *you*?"

"Wait and see what happens next to make your decision," Darius stated. "I wager that the bird is releasing the rat from her cage right about now. You really don't think that ATF wouldn't sacrifice the many for the few?"

"I'm not sure," Lucian responded, "but they don't seem like the type of people to commit mass murder."

"Appearances can be deceiving," Darius said. "You should know that truth firsthand, knowing what happened with Aaron and Evangeline."

"How do you know about them, and how do you know what they did?"

"Why, that's an easy answer," Darius answered, "because I was once one of them."

"A traitor helping another traitor out," Lucian muttered. "How ironic."

"You don't really believe that they'll support your dreams, do you?" Darius asked, his voice growing more sinister. "I, too, was once deceived by the promise of freedom and peace, but not anymore. A new era has arrived, and the old will perish for the sake of the new."

The *pounding* of someone's shoes caught their attention. They looked to see the source: A panicked Angelique ran toward them at full speed. Within a foot or two short of them, she abruptly halted. Panting wildly, she hunched forward and placed her hands on her knees to catch her breath.

In between breaths, she let out the words, "Lorin. Rat. She. Escaped."

"Why, Angelique, how nice of you to join us, or should I call you by your real name?" Darius said, his usually calm expression darkening.

"I don't know what you're talking about," she said, huffing out the words.

"I did say a rat, but you're really a bird, aren't you?" Darius said, eyes burning with rage.

"I just told you that the rat, the traitor, escaped, and you're talking about animals?"

Ignoring her comment, Darius continued to say, "What's that saying you always loved to use? Oh, right! Keep your friends close but your enemies closer. Well, I took a page from your book! So, when did you swap places with her? At the BOTB in Korakk or earlier? When was it, you crafty witch?"

"Can someone please tell me what in Gaia's name is going on!?" Lucian shouted at the top of his lungs.

Angelique stood to her full height and said with a voice that wasn't her own, "Angelique and I swapped places during our attack on the palace several years ago. She was a strong fighter, but not strong enough. If that's all you wanted to know, then let Lucian go."

"No matter how strong the Queen may be," Darius said, "she can't protect her King."

"Stop talking in riddles and tell me what's going on. You're not making any sense."

Darius snapped his fingers. As if a spell was broken, Angelique started to morph into someone else. A familiar face was revealed, a look of sorrow painting her wrinkled face.

"So, Eva, want to tell Lucian what you've been keeping from him—from all of ATF?"

"We weren't lying... We were just—"

"—Just hiding the truth," Darius finished her sentence. "Same tactics. Same lies."

Evangeline stared into Lucian's eyes with a solemn look and said, "I never meant to deceive you, Lucian, and it's the truth that we need you now more than ever."

Darius let out a mocking laugh while saying, "The truth? How hysterical! All you people ever do is seem to lie to unsuspecting souls. Why don't you tell him the *real* truth? That, Lucian isn't the child of prophecy at all! That, you've been lying to him from the start! And that you've been hiding who the real Regulus is all along!"

Lucian felt his world falling apart. Questions started to overflow from his mouth, as he asked, "Why did you lie to me? Who is it? Tell me, Eva! Who's the real Regulus? How are you even here right now?"

Darius spoke in her stead. "Creating clones of herself is a piece of cake for an Illusionary Mage like her. It's nothing to be too surprised about. As for the other question, let's think about the one person who Eva currently doesn't have in her control: the real Regulus. The one who failed to fulfill the prophecy and forced a substitute to shoulder his burden."

"Darius, that's enough," Eva's tone sharpened while saying. "You know very well why I did what I did. It's all for *his* sake, for this kingdom's sake, and for Gaia's sake."

"No, you did this for *yourself*, Evangeline, and you'll soon suffer because of the seeds you've sown."

Making direct eye contact with Lucian, Eva said, in a pleading tone, "Don't let Darius lead you astray, Lucian. I admit that I didn't tell you the whole truth, but it was to prepare as well as to protect you. The prophecy is real! You shall find The Regulus at the end of your journey."

The picture of Aaron popped into Lucian's head.

"Aaron," Lucian let the name slip out.

Continuing with the charade of a conversation, Darius proclaimed, "Don't worry, Lucian. Unlike Eva, I promise that I'll never lie to you! To prove my point, I won't harm a single hair on your head. In return, you'll fulfill your duties and attend the ball as a guard, as planned."

"And if I refuse?" Lucian asked, weighing the captain's words with Eva's excuses.

Curving his lips upward in a wicked smile so chilling that it sent shivers down Lucian's spine, Darius said, "What was that entertainer's name, the one who recently entered the palace before you, Evangeline? Oh, yes, Seraphina. Lucian, if you refuse to attend the ball, then you'll never see her again. No one will ever see her again."

The lights from the festival faded.

A new night had fallen.

17

A PRICE TO PAY

 *Blackridge*

D awn had risen... Rays of sunlight streamed through the shades, revealing the stale, cold room. Dying flames could be heard behind a rusty metal gate, turning into ashes. The welcoming atmosphere the room once had was lost to the eerie silence that hung in the air.

Lighting the dangling illumination crystals, Eva made her way to a seat across from Lucian. Her slightly slouched spine, her deceptively harmless face, and her shuffled steps created the perfect illusion that she was only an elderly woman bound for retirement, but he knew the truth.

"I—" Lucian started saying, but was interrupted by Eva motioning him to wait.

"Not yet, Lucian, we're still waiting for one more person to join us," she said. "I know what you want to ask, and we will explain everything."

Who's "we"?

From the back entrance of the residence, a figure emerged. Wearing a worn-out, white cloak, Angelique appeared, the real Angelique. Quite unlike her former self, she approached them silently and sat next to Eva. Since she wore a neutral expression, he couldn't tell what she was thinking, and that alone made her even more untrustworthy.

Eva extended an introduction, saying, "Angelique, this is the boy from Caelum, Lucian Roux. Lucian, this is The Vice Captain of The Royal Guards, Angelique."

"A pleasure to make your acquaintance," Angelique said with a tempered tone. "I had hoped we would've met under more casual circumstances, but alas..."

Tucking a few loose strands of hair behind her ear, Eva said, "Thank you for coming to speak with us, Lucian. I know we're the last people that you want to see right now, but we wanted to tell you the truth."

The truth? What truth can come out of the mouth of a viper?

Lucian laid his hand on his hilt where Ignis rested, and he said, "Just know that the minute you spout more lies to me, I won't be as cooperative as I am now."

Eva straightened in her seat and said, "First, I must explain to you ATF's true mission."

In response to Eva's actions, Angelique crossed her legs and sat up straight. She retrieved from her cloak a small, weathered notebook and flipped through the pages.

"Lucian, as you learned from Leon, ATF was created not only to safeguard the gods residing in The Earthly Realm but also to free the Fallen gods who have been captured by our true enemy," Eva explained. "The god of illusions, **Akar**."

Out of the recesses of his mind, Lucian responded by saying, "You mean the god who created the pesky Syrases? *That* Akar?"

"Yes, that's right. Felix *did* send a report to us saying that you had a run-in with one of those vile, soul-devouring creatures."

"You mentioned that you're not under the same curse as the gods, but what even *is* the curse?"

Clasping her hands together, she answered, "Eons ago, mankind fought alongside the virtuous gods in a war against the malefic gods over control of The Heavenly Realm and The Earthly Realm. The virtuous gods and the humans won the war, casting the malefic gods into The Fallen Realm. To prevent this same tragedy in the future, The Heavenly Pillars were created, directly connecting The Heavenly Realm to The Earthly Realm. The location of

The Heavenly Pillars in The Earthly Realm, as you're aware, is Caelum. So long as The Heavenly Pillars remained intact, mankind would know that the gods hadn't abandoned them. To ensure that both sides would uphold this promise was a Heavenly Pact. If the pact were to be broken by either side, the price would be a deadly *curse*... A nasty affliction that would corrupt one's body and soul for eternity."

"If Morpheus knew this would happen to the gods, then why did he destroy The Heavenly Pillars?"

"That's the thing," Eva said. "Akar laid a clever trap for the ruling gods of The Heavenly Realm, Adonis and Morpheus. By seizing The Terrasian Throne and causing chaos in the empire, Akar convinced the virtuous gods that the malefic gods had escaped The Fallen Realm, planned to destroy The Earthly Realm, and restored their divine powers confiscated in The Heavenly Realm. Truth be told, Akar was the one who was supposed to cast the malefic gods into The Fallen Realm as punishment for their sins; however, he made a deal with them. In exchange for their allegiance, Akar would lie to the virtuous gods and restore them to their former glory. Unbeknownst to Akar's schemes, Morpheus went to The Earthly Realm and destroyed The Heavenly Pillars, hoping to cut off the malefic gods from restoring their power."

"Aren't the gods supposed to be smart? Why would they fall for such a stupid trick?"

"For centuries, Akar acted as the trusted adviser to Adonis and Morpheus, so he held great authority within The Heavenly Realm. Additionally, he had been assigned to periodically descend to and report about The Earthly Realm. As such, neither Adonis nor Morpheus doubted his claims about the state of The Earthly Realm."

As ridiculous as it all sounded, Lucian remembered everything that he had learned from his travels: Ferris's lectures, Maverick's teachings, and Leon's stories. The fragmented pieces in his mind started to connect.

"Leon said that Akar was motivated by revenge, but, according to your story, that's not the real reason."

Shaking her head, Eva explained, "Revenge is not what *he* seeks. Think about it. What could a god as powerful as Akar gain from destroying the relationship between the twin gods and creating chaos in The Heavenly Realm...?"

"He wanted *control*," Eva said, answering her own question. "Not only that, what he really wanted was..."

A connection formed, and he piped up, saying, "...to be the one, supreme god!"

Akin to the feeling when Master Felix praised him, Lucian's chest filled with pride for connecting the dots. These feelings soon submerged as Angelique spoke up, saying, "Although Akar's silver tongue and illusionary magic are impressive, they're not the 'absolute power' that he needs to control the realms. Unfortunately for us, after years of searching, he found a way." Her voice trailed off, and she looked down at her notebook, referencing the pages.

Angelique laid out Akar's plan to achieve absolute control, explaining, "First, after The Heavenly Pillars were destroyed, Akar plotted to turn the virtuous gods into the Soulless. He used both his Syrases and the seeds from The Tree of Death to turn them into his minions."

Taking a deep breath, she continued, "Second, Akar created the village of Caelum atop the ruins of The Heavenly Pillars. This village served not only as a soul farm to increase his strength but also to restore The Heavenly Pillars."

Blowing a piece of hair out of her face and flipping to a new page in her notebook, she finished, "Third, Akar populated the village of Caelum with children of royal and noble blood who were descendants of the original warriors that fought in the ancient war and had strong connections to the gods. During the so-called Placement Ceremony, he would bind the souls of the gods, who were under his control, into the selected children to create Reincarnates. During the Succession Ceremony, he would activate the godly curse within them and start the process of turning them into members of the Soulless." Angelique paused.

Lucian couldn't believe what he was hearing.

A soul farm in Caelum.

A ceremony that defiled the gods.

"That notebook... How did you get all of this information?"

Flipping through multiple pages, she said, "When I was still under Akar's control, I was The Royal Guard assigned to monitoring Caelum. I learned a lot of nasty secrets while guarding the underground cells. What I've told you is only scratching the surface of the nightmares in that village."

Interrupting the flow of the conversation, Eva interjected and said, "Sorry to cut you off, Angelique, but I'd like to inform Lucian why he was necessary to our mission and what Akar truly wants out of The Harvesting."

Angelique closed her notebook, nodding her head. "I understand, Evangeline. Go ahead."

"Lucian, The Harvesting, as you might have already ascertained, was the final stage in Akar's soul cultivation in Caelum. Once he started The Harvesting, every soul in Caelum was collected and fed to him and The Heavenly Pillars. Unlike previous stages in the process, where he only stole the souls of the Reincarnates, this time, he collected them from the entire village."

"So, what Darius told me about Rosalie being the sole survivor was correct?"

"Honestly, I'm not sure how your sister, Rosalie,

survived other than Akar having other plans for her... which leads me to believe that he spared her life to use her against you."

Questions kept bubbling up, and he asked, "Then, what about the Elders in the village?"

Rubbing her sore shoulder, Eva said, "It's a matter of society building, Lucian. The Elders were kept alive to perform Akar's will to deceive the villagers. The Elders, however, weren't perfect, so Akar's trusted minion, who can manipulate memories, was needed."

So that's who the prophecy was referring to...

"Okay, so I understand that Akar is a greedy god who wants to be above all other gods," Lucian started to say, "but what does that have to do with Aaron and me?"

Moving from rubbing her shoulder to her temples, Eva explained, "Akar is no exception to the effects of the pact. He too suffers from the degradation of his body and his soul while residing in The Earthly Realm. That's why he needed a vessel that could not only resist the curse but also contain the soul of a god. While he collected the souls of Reincarnates, he also used them as test subjects to see if they were compatible with the souls of lesser and higher gods. Among the gods whom he controlled, the souls of Morpheus and Adonis were too powerful to be contained in human vessels, until he tried placing them into Aaron and you."

"Wait, Aaron is Adonis's Reincarnate?" He blurted out, the color draining from his face. "But the Var proclaimed Elias Daye as his Reincarnate!"

"If you've learned anything from what I've told you about Akar, it's that he likes to lie," she said. "You can't trust a single word that comes out of his mouth. Elias Daye was just a placeholder until Aaron came completely under his control. Unfortunately for Akar, Aaron's body was deemed unfit to be his vessel, since he couldn't, no, wouldn't unlock the last ability that was required for a successful resurrection: *Manipulation*. No matter how hard Akar tried, he couldn't force Aaron to access Adonis's full power. Therefore, Aaron was deemed defective."

"So that's why I was chosen..." Lucian lamented. "And because I fled, everyone in my village is dead. What have I done..."

Standing up and crossing the room, Eva cupped his face between her hands, and she said, "No, Lucian, because you left, we have a chance to defeat him. The Harvesting would've taken place after your Succession Ceremony with or without you...and it did. Since our numbers dwindled during the failed attack several years ago, we could only rely on the insider that we sent to Caelum. So, don't blame yourself. It's not your fault."

Tears welled in his eyes. All of his life, he wanted to hear those words, "It isn't your fault." However, now was neither the time nor the place to lick his wounds and drown in his sorrows. He shook his head. Releasing his face from her hands, he wiped his tears on his sleeve.

With the mention of the insider lingering in his head, Lucian asked, "The insider?"

"Yes," Eva said, "we sent your stepmother, Melinda, into Caelum..."

Memories of Melinda weaved their way into his head, as he remembered her strange looks, silences, and conversations with him. He also remembered the incident with Master Felix's parcel and how that drove a wedge between his father and his stepmother.

"We sent her to Caelum to stall The Harvesting for as long as possible," Eva explained. "And to alert us when she thought the process would begin, so we could save you in time. However, Akar knew about her too. That's why we had to send Aaron to rescue you in her stead. She was supposed to be your savior and our spy."

"She was a sacrifice?" Lucian asked, befuddled. "What mortal can rival a god?"

Changing the course of the conversation, Eva pointed at Lucian, saying, "You, my boy."

"How am I supposed to defeat him if everyone else has failed?" he asked, gripping his thigh tightly with his hand.

"You must use everything that he wants from you against him," she said, removing the mana-restricting bracelets from his wrists. "The god residing within you is one of the most powerful souls in all of the realms. Draw on *his* strength, and *he* will guide you to victory. Even Adonis, the god of creation, can't undo the damage caused by Morpheus, the god of destruction. Use his power, and you'll succeed."

Amid the serious conversation, a familiar voice rose to say, "I, too, would be honored to slice that dastardly god up into bite-sized pieces, Lucian. If not Morpheus, then trust in me, your clever, handsome, and bright sword!"

Lucian felt comforted as he heard the voice of his one-and-only sword, Ignis. Upon entering The Terras Empire, he foresaw images of an epic battle at the palace, but not like this.

As trusting as Lucian had been in the past, he warned them, "Just know that I'm not the same child I was when I started this journey. You'd better prepare me properly for the battle to come. While I want to save Rosalie and Seraphina, this doesn't mean that I trust you fully, not anymore."

Patting him on the shoulder, Eva said, "I shall keep that in mind."

Letting out a fake cough, Angelique asked, "So, shall we get started?"

18

KNIGHT, KING, KNAVE

 *Blackridge*

The clicking of her heels on the wooden floor drove Lucian mad. Angelique paced back and forth, running through the plan for the fifth time in a row. His head hurt, as he thought of all the things that could go wrong. Even with Ignis's encouragement, he felt sick to his stomach.

Wearing a frilly, cream-colored suit, Lucian looked closer to a spoiled noble than a Royal Guard. The neckline and sleeves had pure-white lace accentuating them. Golden pins lined the front of the fit. He honestly felt like a fool wearing such fancy clothes.

"Remember to wear your ring," Angelique ordered. "Eva told me that the ring already has a protection spell, so she went ahead and added a teleportation spell. However, it's only a one-time-use spell, so make sure you activate it if the plan goes awry."

"Yeah, yeah, I know," he dismissively said, slipping on the ornate ring. "Are you sure that I don't have to wear the earrings? Aren't I supposed to still be 'The Royal Guard, Ashton?'"

"Your identity has already been compromised," Angelique stated, "so there's no need."

His slicked-back blond hair shone in the sun rays trickling in from the window. Ruffling the strands to his liking, he stood straight up, tying all the loose knots and buttons on his outfit. He wore a golden chain around his neck with a miniature-sized sword as the pendant. As he motioned to put Master Felix's scepter into his pocket from his stack of belongings, Angelique snatched it from him.

"You can't bring weapons into the palace, remember?" she said, sternly.

Tugging on the chain, he retorted, "And *this* isn't considered a weapon?"

Sticking the chain under his collar, she said, "So long as you don't wave the thing around like that, it won't be. You should thank Eva for casting a cloaking spell on Ignis to miniaturize him. If she hadn't, then you would've gone in barehanded. Are you ready yet?"

"Yes, mother dearest," he sarcastically said.

Eva's acting as Angelique wasn't too far off the mark, he thought, smirking to himself.

Ignis replied, emphatically, "You got that right!"

Nice to know someone's on my side...

"Sure am... After all, we are bound by a contract."

So, you're stuck with me? Great...

Hearing the clock strike four, Angelique started swarming around like an agitated bee. She fixed her hair for the ninth time, slipped on her silk shawl, and grabbed his hand, leading him out the door to the carriage. Everything went so fast that he didn't even have time to think about anything except how itchy his outfit was as he walked.

Plopped on a cushion within the carriage, the horses lurched forward with gusto. Knowing what was to come, he went over the plan for the last time in his head: *First, Angelique is going to create a distraction after the first dance and save Seraphina. Second, using the blueprints, I'm going to find where the black fumes are coming from and destroy the source. Third, I'm going to escape through the portal in the underground cells back to the ATF headquarters. As a backup plan, if anything goes awry, I'll use the ring to tele-port away to safety. While this plan is being executed, Lawrence will save his sister at the headquarters of The Royal Guards.*

Somewhere in the back of his head, however, Lucian knew something wrong was bound to happen. After all, none of the plans that he or anyone else created for him ever ended up working out. Tapping his fingers on the side of the carriage, he tried taking his mind off the mission. During the thirty-minute ride, he distracted himself with thoughts of the different delicacies and desserts that would be displayed for consumption.

Drool started pooling in his mouth.

Minute by minute, the scenery slowly changed outside. The streets seemed to grow narrower, the lights seemed to burn brighter, and the air seemed to feel colder. Before he had time to breathe in these changes, they arrived at The Terrasian Palace. Having previously seen the palace from the top of the fortress, Lucian was amazed by the sheer size of the structure. He had been left speechless many times before by Lunarian and Avrithian architecture, but this structure was on a whole other scale.

The towers sitting atop and beside the structure looked like sharpened knives, all aiming up toward The Heavenly Realm. Cold light streamed out of the thin, rectangular windows that stretched unusually long like glue. Flocks of crows swarmed around the tops of the towers, as they cawed at the guests. Whether their caws were a welcome or a warning, Lucian knew not.

As he escorted Angelique out of the carriage, she remarked to him, "Don't soil your pants, kiddo. We haven't even seen the enemy yet."

Flustered, he stuttered out the words, "I-I would never."

She slapped him on the back while saying, "Lighten up, Lucian. It was just a joke."

Not a very funny joke...

Queuing with the other guests, they passed through security. Several guards checked their belongings and bodies for weapons of any kind. In addition, since it was supposedly a masquerade ball, they were each given a special mask to wear, which hid the upper portion of their face. The mask given to Lucian was adorned with black feathers and red glitter. Very unfitting colors for his all-white outfit; however, he was in no position to complain or to care.

Pretending to be escorted, Angelique led him into the palace, following the swarm of nobles, who chattered and sauntered toward the ballroom. Glancing at his surroundings, Lucian noticed the opulence of the space. Diamond chandeliers fixed with illumination crystals, silk drapes, and blue-pigmented paintings, greatly contrasted the poverty in the rest of the empire.

Angelique nudged him while saying, "Stop making that face. You'll blow our cover."

Taking in a deep breath, his facial expression turned from a deep frown to a forced smile. Itching to clear his conscience, he said in a lower tone than normal, "Once we defeat him, can we burn this building down?"

She retorted, "I'll bring the wood. But for now, let's focus first on fulfilling our part of the plan. The better we do, the easier it'll be for Lawrence to save Lorin."

Tugging Angelique closer, Lucian said, in an even softer tone, "You said that you'd tell me today what distraction you'll pull in the ballroom. I'm very curious to see it."

She winked at him while saying, "All you have to remember is that once you hear any sort of commotion, you need to slip out of the ballroom. Timing is everything, after all. Evangeline and I understand that we're walking straight into a trap, but how else could we access the palace so easily? Lucian, I trust that you won't fail us."

Smoothing a strand of loose hair, he responded, "Sure, let's hope that Darius sticks with his end of the promise. He promised that I wouldn't be harmed if I attended."

With a lower tone and a serious look on her face, Angelique said, "Darius is a man of his word. Even when he switched sides to serve The Royal Guards, he boldly declared his departure to Evangeline without resorting to spying."

"Loyalty, bravery, camaraderie," he recited. "I wonder what really happened to him..."

When his partner didn't respond to his recitation, he realized the plan had already begun. They entered the ballroom behind a noble couple wearing a set of lavish outfits with peacock feathers sprouting from the lower-back fabric. Lucian swallowed his anxieties, laying his hand on his chest where Ignis resided.

Descending the grand staircase, Lucian scanned the room, trying to recognize Darius by his bulky build alone. When they reached the bottom of the stairs, Angelique seemed to locate him first. Purposefully positioning themselves for Darius to notice their arrival, the plan started. Angelique gracefully greeted passersby, who complimented their masks and outfits. She seemed to take the compliments more gracefully than Lucian, as he was a stranger to flattery.

I feel more comfortable with people cursing at me than speaking this shallow fluff...

"Here he comes," Angelique acknowledged. "Let me deal with him, as planned."

Gulping down his nerves, Lucian nodded in agreement.

Darius weaved through the crowd, reaching them without resistance. Regal and proud, the captain stood before them without the slightest crack in his smile. He wore a cream-colored suit with golden shoulder paddings and tassels. The cuffs of his sleeves were green and gold with intricately woven threads. Adorning his left shoulder, the same fabric on his chest created a regal cape that fell to the floor. The chest region was also green with an elaborate leaf pattern lining the outfit. The entire fit looked like it had been crafted through delicate lacework.

Resting his hand on Lucian's right shoulder, Darius said, "I see that I'm not the only man who keeps my word in the empire. Nice to see you, Lucian, and you too, Angelique."

Shortly after the greeting, the first song commenced. Releasing her arm from Lucian's, Angelique extended her hand out to Darius, who recognized her unspoken intentions. The burly man let out a laugh and bowed his head to her, accepting her dance proposal. They locked arms with each other and went out to the dance floor. Lucian retreated to the sidelines where he waited for his signal to perform his part.

He watched as Angelique and Darius danced effortlessly across the marble floor. Their dance captivated the audience, who were entranced with eyes glued to them in envy and awe. Truly, they were as regal as they were lethal. They were so amusing that Lucian was easily caught off guard. A pair of hands grasped his shoulders from behind and wouldn't release him. The perpetrator's nails dug into him.

"Why did you come here?" a small voice asked with a tone as soft as a mouse. "You shouldn't have come. If he sees you, then you'll never be able to escape him. Run while you still can...while I can still maintain control of myself."

Grabbing onto the hands that tore into him, Lucian ripped them off his shoulders and turned around to face the speaker. Expecting to see Seraphina, his jaw dropped open to see someone who made his heart stop for a split second. Solely by her silver hair, he recognized her almost immediately. It was his one-and-only younger sister, Rosalie.

"Rosalie, I'm so sorry," he whispered while leading Rosalie away into a hidden corner. "If I knew, then I would've—"

"What were you supposed to do? Die with the rest of the village? Nothing would've changed even if you had stayed with us. Our entire family would've died, anyway."

Copying Eva's movements, Lucian cupped his sister's cheeks between his hands while saying, "If I could turn back time, then I would've never abandoned you or our family. I should've stayed and died in Caelum. I should've never trusted Aaron, that dirty liar. But we can't turn back time. All I can do is give you this pitiful apology, but know that I'm sincerely sorry for not protecting you."

"This is why I can't hate you," she said while fighting back tears. "Lucian, this is my final warning to you. Escape now, before he finds you and traps your soul. Once you're in his sights, he won't let you go. No matter where you hide or how far you run, *he'll* find you. Please, leave, Lucian, before the tragedy repeats itself. Be free."

"Freedom without family and friends isn't freedom at all," he said to her, softly stroking her silver strands. "I want to protect you, no matter where I may go, whether it be the heights of The Heavenly Realm or the endless furnaces of The Fallen Realm. Trust me, Rosalie, I'll save you. We'll be free."

Interrupting their tears, a shrill cry broke through the merry mood of the ballroom. Coming from the direction where Darius and Angelique were dancing, Lucian knew that this disruption was his cue. Before he went, he mouthed the words, "I'm sorry," to her.

Releasing Rosalie from his hold, Lucian raced toward the side exit, slipping past gawking nobles and paralyzed waiters. Seeing a few flashes of the incident through the openings in the crowd, Angelique's fallen figure burned in his vision. He tore his attention away from her, reminding himself of his part in the plan.

Just hold on until this is all over, Rosalie. Your big brother isn't going to run away anymore. I'll save you as I promised, and we'll find true freedom together as a family.

Bursting through the side exit, Lucian ran straight into someone, the impact knocking his mask right off his face. The force pushed him backward. Disoriented but desperate, he regained his balance and sprinted past the figure.

While passing, he heard a chilling cackle, one that he instantly recognized from years of torment surfacing from his memory. He stopped in his tracks, turning back to ascertain the figure who taunted him. A bejeweled crown sat snuggly on the young man's head. His eyes were as cold as ice. A smug smirk lifted the young man's lips, and he said, "And where do you think you're going, filthy commoner? I suppose some things never change, do they, Lucian?"

Eyes widened and mouth ajar, Lucian seethed at the familiar figure while responding, "How are you alive, Elias? Aren't you supposed to be dead?"

Pointing the royal scepter at Lucian's chest, Elias proudly proclaimed, "That's Emperor Elias to you. I am Akar's chosen vessel, so evading death is child's play. You managed to escape us once, but never again."

"Chosen vessel?" Lucian mockingly laughed at him while saying, "Do you really think Akar wants a broken urn like you? You're merely a substitute."

Enraged, Elias swung his scepter at Lucian's head and screamed with spit flying out of his mouth, "Akar is the only god that matters. His ways are indiscernible to us humans, so I can't fathom why he chose someone like you. But don't get too cocky. Once he deems you unworthy, he'll realize that *I* am the only one who can serve as his vessel."

I swear this jerk is so stupid!

"I don't have time for your crazy rambling!" Lucian shouted. "Go and be Akar's vessel all you want. I have more important things to do!"

Assuming a serene facial expression, Elias snickered while saying, "Oh, you mean that pitiful excuse for a distraction? Let me tell you something, Lucian. No one in this castle needs saving. At least, not who you're thinking about, not Seraphina."

Tightening his fist, Lucian stated, "I don't know what you mean, but I won't listen to the words of a liar—a snake."

"Say what you will, but you really should be more careful with whom you choose to trust," Elias said, twirling his scepter in his hand. "I wasn't supposed to tell you this, but you just look so pitiful. Weren't you aware that Seraphina was betraying you all along? That she was our spy feeding us information about you from the start?"

"That's not true," Lucian denied. "Seraphina would never do such a thing!"

Elias's lips curved upward as he said, "Well, I wouldn't be too sure of that. None of the gods within The Earthly Realm is outside of *his* influence, not even Seraphina's precious Leon. You really don't think that she would betray you to keep Leon safe when his soul could be easily extinguished?"

Lucian latched onto his chain, tearing it off his neck. Yelling Ignis's name, the sword morphed into his full form. Lucian pointed the tip of the blade at Elias, conjuring red-and-blue flames.

"A futile effort," Elias said while snapping his fingers. Ignis's flames were instantly extinguished. "Can't you see that you're not in any position to negotiate? Give up!"

"I will never give up!" Lucian said while lurching forward and swinging the sword at Elias with full force. "Not until the black fumes are extinguished, my friends are saved, and Akar is defeated. I will never let evil win."

Stopping the swing with his bare hand, Elias said, "Idiots like you never learn, I swear. Well, those black fumes that you're so adamant about extinguishing are coming from Caelum, so I guess I should send you on your way. Besides, an old friend of yours is waiting for you."

With a wicked smile, Elias held his scepter in the air and slapped it on the side of Lucian's body. Too quick for Lucian to react, he was pushed backward into a summoned portal.

Elias's last words left a bitter taste in Lucian's mouth: "Losers never win. That's just the way the world works. Resent your bad luck, little Lucian."

Without any footing, Lucian fell onto his backside. The portal disappeared, leaving him stranded in a land that stank of burning flesh and sulfur. He plugged his nose with his fingers, wiping the dust and dirt out of his eyes. As Elias said, Lucian found himself in his hometown, the one place that haunted him.

The crunch of rubble filled his ears as someone was steadily approaching.

From the black fog emerged the figure of his former friend, the one who originally betrayed his trust and the members of ATF, Aaron Knight.

19

A FIGHT FOR FREEDOM

 *Caelum*

Y ou should've stayed dead." Aaron towered over him. Looking up to meet his eyes, Lucian noticed a clear difference in Aaron's demeanor. Unlike in The Terras Mountains, Aaron's bloodshot and weary eyes expressed conflicting emotions: regret, anger, disappointment, and desperation. At this moment, anyone would've thought Aaron was the *real* victim.

Gripping the gravel beneath his palms, Lucian retorted by saying, "You should've killed me back at the inn when you had the chance."

After Lucian said those words, a guilty expression formed on his former comrade's face.

Pressing him further, Lucian asked, "Isn't it ironic that

you're the one who betrayed me this time around? We're a product of our pasts, aren't we, Reincarnate of Adonis?"

Aaron didn't respond.

Shooting straight up, Lucian grabbed onto his collar and shook him while shouting, "Say something, you traitor! Or am I not worth your time anymore since I'm just a sacrifice? Can't harm the merchandise, can you?"

Taking on the full brunt of Lucian's rage, Aaron refused to budge. His feet were firmly planted on the floor, and his eyes were emotionless. After unleashing a whole year's worth of rage, Lucian released Aaron and threw him to the ground. Aaron just lay there, appearing as a mere silhouette of his former self. No snarky comments. No angry outbursts. The silence was then interrupted by a fit of coughing. Bits of black blood bubbled up from Aaron's stomach and drizzled out of his mouth.

Propping himself on his elbow, Aaron wiped the blood from his face and rhetorically asked, "Are you satisfied yet, you stupid sacrifice?"

"What did you say!?"

Lucian lunged at him, but he stopped himself. Aaron clearly wasn't in a state to fight. Although Aaron was his archenemy, Lucian couldn't force himself to take advantage of his weakness. Lucian vowed that he'd never stoop to Aaron's level, so he waited for him to speak.

"Why couldn't I kill you...?" Aaron rambled, burying

his face in his hands. "I knew you would be chosen as Akar's next vessel if I failed my mission, so why couldn't I go through with it? I should've been the only sacrifice."

"What nonsense are you spouting? Are you saying that I was going to be sacrificed either way? Just because you failed? I trusted you! You were my first friend!"

Aaron burst out into laughter while saying, "If only you didn't forget me like the fool you are! All of those years that my mother and I suffered in The Terras Empire...I held on to the hope that you would remember!"

"What are you talking about? Stop spouting nonsense! I'm sick of you lying to me! Curses and prophecies, what good are they when your own friends betray you and sacrifice you to the gods?"

Without warning, Aaron jumped up and unsheathed Phantom. As fast as lightning, he plunged his blade at Lucian. Not expecting the attack, Lucian tried to block it with his hands. Fortunately, Aerus's protection remained impenetrable and shielded Lucian from the attack. Aaron's sword hit the barrier, unable to even leave a scratch on him.

Escaping his lips, Aaron let out a *Tch!* sound.

In the instance that Aerus protected him, Lucian unsheathed his own sword, Ignis, and retreated several feet away from Aaron. Not even the slightest bit surprised that Aaron would use such a scummy trick, Lucian readied himself for battle.

Refuting Aaron's previous words, Lucian yelled, "While I don't remember the promise we made, I can assure you that I never would've signed up to be a sacrifice!"

"If it were the old you, we wouldn't even be having this conversation."

The old me?

Closing the gap between them, Aaron swung his sword again at Lucian. The momentum of his attack pushed Lucian's body back. Lucian dug his heels in the dirt to resist the force, conjuring up all of the strength that he could.

Sword clashing against sword, Lucian and Aaron haphazardly threw all of their aggression at each other. Right or wrong, they were fighting with sheer willpower and brute strength. Even as they sliced at each other's bodies, they refused to stop. Screaming out crude curses and insults, they fought like animals.

"Answer me, Aaron, was everything a lie!?"

"Shut up! Just die already!"

Aaron's transformation into a Soulless was weakening him. He fumbled and stumbled more than usual. Even without using Ignis at full strength, Lucian was stronger than Aaron, far exceeding him in both power and speed.

After knocking Aaron to the ground again, Lucian hovered over him with his blade pointed at his neck.

Glaring at him, Lucian said, "I'm not the weak boy you once knew."

Cracking a resigned smile, Aaron dropped his sword and held his hands in the air. "I concede."

"It's not like you to admit defeat so easily," Lucian stated. "What do you want from me?"

"Well, let's just say I have other plans for you," Aaron responded.

"And what might those plans be?"

"I want you to succeed where I failed."

"You're not making any sense. You just told me that you wanted me dead. Several times, for that matter."

"I was testing you, and you passed with flying colors."

"I could kill you right now, and you're blabbering about some test?"

Shaking his raven-colored head, Aaron said, "I needed to know if you were ready for your final mission. If I deemed you weren't ready, then I would've tried to defeat Akar alone. But you can see my current state. I don't have much time left. You're *our* only hope. Even if you don't remember me, I trust that you'll always keep your word and save your friends."

"What are you talking about?" Lucian sighed while saying. "Aren't you the least afraid that I'll slit your throat right here and now?"

"I am confident that neither the old Lucian nor the

new one would take a life. You were the one who always used to say that you didn't want to end up like your father. Do you really think you can snuff out someone's life without bearing the consequences?"

"Why should I trust anything you're saying?"

"Don't trust me, Lucian. Trust yourself and your friends who have supported you."

What good are my so-called friends if they always lie to me?

Cautiously retrieving something from his neck, Aaron threw a small and shiny object at him. Grabbing the object out of the air, Lucian realized what it was: the stone from the barrier. The fiery red color sparkled despite the overcast skies. For a split second, he could see Eteria's reflection in the stone. Relieved to see her face, he hastily tied the pendant back around his neck.

"That's what the prophecy was referring to," Aaron said, spitting out more bits of black blood. "Well, it's one of them, at least. You need both of the *hearts* to restore the connection between the realms."

"What even are these *hearts*?"

"The *hearts* are the keys..." Aaron said, breathing unevenly. "The barrier stone from Caelum is the *first* heart. The *second* heart is in The Fallen Realm, so I need you to retrieve it. Only when the two *hearts* become one can the evil one be defeated."

Not this crap again... Lucian thought, rolling his eyes.

"Who died and made you king?" Lucian asked, sarcastically.

Genuinely laughing at Lucian's question, Aaron cryptically replied, "Well, that's a story for another day. Regardless, Akar will be here any moment. I was ordered to stall you long enough until he arrived, so I guess we both ended up with what we wanted from this ordeal."

"What do you—"

"Listen closely, Lucian," Aaron said, cutting Lucian off. "I'm going to open the gateway to The Fallen Realm. Once you're in that realm, you'll need to follow the stone. It'll resonate when it senses its twin."

"Not a chance."

Lucian walked over to Aaron, kicking his Phantom sword to the side, just to be on the safe side. Picking him up, Lucian threw Aaron over his shoulder like a sack of potatoes. Even though they had fought like children earlier, Aaron surprisingly lay still on his shoulder.

"What do you think you're doing right now? We don't have time for you to stall any longer. You need to go to The Fallen Realm and retrieve the stone before Akar returns and forces you to become his vessel."

"Screw you. Screw the prophecy. Screw Akar," Lucian sharply said. "I don't have time for you or your idiocy. Since you're so concerned about the *hearts*, I'm taking you with me. Don't try to escape, or else I'll knock you unconscious."

Raising his right hand in front of him, Lucian looked at the ring in which Eva had so kindly placed the teleportation spell. After he recited the ancient words, he quickly realized the spell wasn't working. Shaking his hand rapidly, he kept reciting the spell, but the results remained the same.

"Why isn't it working? Did Angelique lie to me? I knew I shouldn't have trusted them."

"I see that you're not completely stupid since you had a backup plan. Unfortunately, that spell you tried to cast only works if the portal at the destination you're trying to travel to is active."

A surge of panic seized Lucian.

"It was supposed to teleport me from anywhere in Gaia back to the ATF headquarters. Does that mean that the portal has been destroyed?"

"I assume so," Aaron said in a matter-of-fact tone. "Now, are you ready to listen to me?"

"Shut up, you stupid summoner."

"No matter where you try to run, Akar will find you. Why can't you understand we're in a race against time? The Fallen Realm is the only safe spot for you since Akar can't freely enter."

Amid their bantering, a portal appeared out of thin air,

and Elias stepped out of it. The cocky expression that he usually wore was nowhere in sight. The slight curl of Elias's lips reminded Lucian of the Var's cruel smile at the Succession Ceremony years ago.

"I'm disappointed in you, Aaron. You were defeated so easily, but I guess even *you* can't hold a candle to my new vessel," Elias said. "I'm tired of wearing this weak skin. I can't wait to be finally free."

"*Akar*," Aaron spat out the words.

"I thought Elias was too weak to be your vessel, Akar," Lucian said in disbelief.

Crossing his arms, Akar replied, "He *is* too weak. I can't even surface for more than a few minutes without his body starting to break. That's why I'm so excited to see you, Lucian, my precious and perfect vessel."

The Elias who stood before them wasn't the annoying bully from his village anymore. His soul had been seized by the evil god, Akar, and Lucian knew that they would lose if they tried to fight him. Aaron's condition was rapidly declining, and Lucian wasn't confident that he could defeat an ancient god even with Ignis's and Morpheus's help during the fight.

"What are the words?" Lucian asked Aaron in a soft whisper. "Tell me, *now*."

In an equally low tone, Aaron answered, "*Ne nos in terra ceciderunt*."

Firmly grasping onto the chain, Lucian recited the incantation, "*Ne nos in terra ceciderunt!*"

A black hole appeared beneath them.

Elias's expression twisted into rage as he screamed out the words, "Curse you, Morpheus! Curse you, Adonis!"

Falling deeper and deeper, Lucian kept a tight hold on Aaron. If he were to descend into the darkness, then he refused to fall alone. He was so sick and tired of everyone sending him on solo missions, gods-knows-where, without an end in sight. This time, Lucian was the rule maker.

The further they fell, the more reality hit Lucian where they were headed...

The Fallen Realm.

20

THE FALLEN REALM

Two voices merged. One was that of a young woman; the other one was that of a young man. They seemed to be bickering with each other. A chorus of voices joined the conversation along with an annoying, familiar voice.

Lucian could barely think, let alone speak, so he waited until his mind cleared.

Slowly regaining mental clarity and awareness, Lucian thought to himself, *What's going on? Where am I? Who's whining so much?*

Cracking his eyes open, he could barely make out five figures standing off in the distance. One of the figures held a lantern that emitted a tiny flame, flickering back and forth.

Their muffled voices became clearer as time went on. One of the figures happened to notice his gaze. What seemed to be a shorter shadow approached him.

Rising from the floor, Lucian stood upright. Looking around, there was nothing but complete and utter darkness. Aside from the puny light that lit up the immediate surroundings, everything else was shrouded. This darkness didn't appear to be like the dark of night, but rather it reminded him of his nightmares.

Squinting his eyes to see the figure approaching him, he realized just how short they were. Noticing that he was on guard, the figure slowed down their pace while taking off their hood. Although shadows obscured most of the figure's face, Lucian was sure of who it was.

It had to be *her*.

"Is that really you, Seraphina?"

Pulling him into a hug, she said, "Of course, it's me, Lucian. I'm so glad you're safe."

"To be completely honest, I wish we weren't. I mean, isn't this place The Fallen Realm?" Lucian said, cracking a light joke.

"Ah, you're right, I misspoke... Anyway, we should regroup with the others."

Locking her hands with his, they walked toward the

four figures in the distance. He stared down at their hands, thinking, *Maybe she didn't betray me, after all.*

The low light grew brighter with each step, and the faces of the figures slowly started to come into view. Arriving at the makeshift campsite, Lucian couldn't believe *who* was there. Aside from Seraphina and Lucian, the other figures standing in front of him were Aaron, Aerus, Eteria, and Master Felix. It was surprising enough that Aerus and Eteria took their physical forms. Even more so, he was befuddled at Master Felix's presence after his stunt in Orsus.

"What are you—"

Finishing his sentence for him, Master Felix answered, "—doing here? Well, that's a long story, and we don't have that much time to play catch-up."

"Don't be so short with him," Eteria whined, clinging to Master Felix like a lovebird. "We haven't all seen him in a while, so we should celebrate."

"Now's not the time to celebrate, Eteria," Aerus warned. "That fiend won't wait forever before he decides to unleash chaos on the surface. We must retrieve the second heart."

Making a funny face, she replied, "Aerus, you're no fun, but I guess that's what happens when you spend a few centuries stuck inside an inanimate object."

In an awkward tone, Master Felix urged, "Let's calm

down, everyone. I think we should update Lucian on our current situation."

Albeit perceivably pouting, Eteria agreed.

Refusing to give up, Lucian interjected, "I don't think we should proceed with this plan until you explain to me how this meeting is even happening."

In a perky tone, Seraphina said, "I can explain!"

"No," Lucian said. "Master Felix, you need to explain everything... About your fake identity, your disappearance in Caelum, and your lack of contact for years. *Everything*."

Walking closer to Lucian and placing his hand on Lucian's shoulder, Master Felix said, in a serious tone, "Lucian, it's not that I didn't want to contact you or hide my identity, but you must know that I made these decisions for your safety and well-being."

"Let's see, my one-and-only mentor decided to disappear and abandon me," Lucian argued. "I'm not sure how you can so brazenly say that everything was for my safety. I'm curious to hear what lame excuse you have for not contacting me. Go on. Say it to my face."

"It's because I'm Morpheus," Master Felix revealed.

Lucian stopped to think about what Master Felix said for several seconds. As he came to terms with the truth, confusion turned to rage and burst to the surface.

"Is this some sort of sick joke? That's impossible! You can't be Morpheus. I would know since that pesky god has been living inside of me my entire life. Are you trying to piss me off?" Lucian exclaimed, raving like a madman. "Does that mean Leon was lying to me, too?"

Lucian turned to look at Aaron, hoping for support from someone who should've understood his struggles. But the effort bore no fruit, as Aaron replied, "He's right, you know. At first, I thought you were playing dumb with me out of spite, but it became crystal clear that you didn't remember his true identity when you kept referring to him as 'Master Felix' instead of Morpheus. I wasn't aware of how much of your memories Akar had rewritten."

My memories... Akar messed with my memories?

Continuing with the explanation, Master Felix said, "As for why you can see the physical forms of Aerus and Eteria, the only explanation is because of *where* we are, The Fallen Realm. This realm, unlike the other two realms, specifically deals with matters related to souls. You technically don't need to have a physical body in The Fallen Realm to exist. As for me, my case is a little different. Because of my ability to split off a piece of my soul, I can materialize in my physical form even within The Earthly Realm."

"You're not making any sense," Lucian stated. "If what you're saying is true, then why didn't you just stay in your physical form at all times?"

Scratching his head, his mentor replied, "Easier said

than done, Lucian. I'm not all-powerful, so I relied on the energy from The Heavenly Pillars to sustain me. When you left Caelum, I had to draw from my strength alone, so saving you from the Syras and training you for those two weeks in Orsus came with a hefty cost. That's why I could only reach out to you through your dreams or your thoughts."

"How do you explain all of those times when you talked about revenge and death and those stories about you and Leon in The Academy?" Lucian asked, raising his brow. "Were any of those stories real? Don't tell me you're actually an evil god..."

Waving his hands in front of him, Master Felix explained, "No, no! That wasn't me. You see, a part of my soul is under *his* control, which *he* corrupted. Those evil thoughts that you heard were from *him*, not me. As for Leon, I told him to create a realistic backstory that would fool anyone who asked. I can't believe that he told the stories to you, though. When I was Ferris, Master Maverick did the same."

"Okay...let's say I believe you. What's the connection to Caelum?" Lucian asked, tilting his head to the side.

"As you're already aware, within Caelum lies the ruins of The Heavenly Pillars, which is the closest connection to The Heavenly Realm," Master Felix explained, regaining his composure. "Even though The

Heavily Pillars were destroyed, the connection wasn't completely severed. That's why the Elders of Caelum can live for such a long time, and as I said, that's how I was able to draw enough power to maintain my physical form."

After hearing his explanation, Lucian apologized by saying, "I'm sorry for yelling at you, Master Felix."

Ruffling Lucian's blond strands, Master Felix said, "As long as you know my absence wasn't intentional."

Looking to the side, Lucian noticed that Seraphina was intently listening to their conversation. Seraphina's presence reminded him of Leon.

Shifting the subject, Lucian asked, "If this is some special space for ancient gods, then where is Leon, and why was he able to stay in his physical form in The Earthly Realm?"

"Two main things are working in Leon's favor, Lucian," Master Felix said. "First, Leon is the god of restoration. Due to the nature of his powers, his soul has a stronger resistance to curses, but even he can't fully nullify the curse's effects. Second, Leon is, by nature, one of the gods of The Earthly Realm, so his soul is more acclimated to that realm, unlike Adonis and me, who are gods of The Heavenly Realm."

The cogs in Lucian's head started to turn, but he couldn't understand everything at once. He sat in silence for a few moments, trying to figure out how everything connected.

Letting out a nasty cough, Aaron said, "I'm sorry for interrupting you since you look deep in thought, but can we please move the plan along? I'd like to live and die as a human and not as a Soulless, thank you very much."

Aerus, who rarely spoke, decided to take charge of the conversation to explain the plan to Lucian. Seeing Lucian's confusion, Aerus first mentioned the basic structures of The Three Realms. "You see, Lucian, every realm has a ruler or a set of rulers who manage the day-to-day affairs. However, there are entities above the rulers called 'The High Judges.' Their primary duty is to serve as the final word between gods during times of conflict. In exchange for their authority, their souls are bound to their respective realm."

Thinking back to his visions, Lucian vaguely remembered The High Judge of The Heavenly Realm, who openly disagreed with Morpheus's decision to destroy The Heavenly Pillars to save The Earthly Realm. Although Lucian only heard the voice of The High Judge, he gathered that the entity was larger than life.

Aerus then spoke of the dilemma that they would inevitably face when trying to retrieve the second stone. "The second stone is currently in the hands of The High Judge of The Fallen Realm, who is less judicious and more mischievous than his counterparts. Knowing how he operates, in exchange for the second stone, one of our souls will serve as the price."

For once in his life, Lucian didn't ask any questions. Instead, he carefully listened to Aerus's well-crafted plan, even though Lucian vehemently disagreed with the sacrifice that had to be made. Out of all the members, Aerus chose to sacrifice his soul to The High Judge. As the god of protection, Aerus explained that it was time for his era as a god to end. Turning back into a raw soul, according to him, wouldn't be the worst thing to happen to him.

"About Aaron..." Lucian changed topics. "Are we sure that he's not going to turn into a Soulless before we retrieve the second stone? His condition was very *dire* on the surface."

Shooting daggers in his direction, Aaron sarcastically said, "I'm *so* sorry that I fell into Akar's trap and allowed him to worsen the curse."

"What do you mean?"

"Are you seriously going to make me explain myself to you?" Aaron asked, half-angrily and half-seriously. "We can't delay this mission any longer. We'll talk on the way. While we're on the subject, Lucian, you'll have to support me. My condition is worse than I thought."

Even in human form, Aaron's still a tyrant...

After Lucian started supporting Aaron on his shoulder

while walking, Aaron explained, "There are two ways that a Soulless is created: Either by the curse or The Tree of Death. In the case of the curse, the more that a Reincarnate draws on his or her predecessor's godly powers, the worse the curse becomes. In my case, since I refused to use my powers, Akar forced me down the second scenario when he forced me to consume a seed from The Tree of Death. The seed's nourishment is from one's soul."

So that's what it was...

Even as time passed, the scenery stayed the same. Lucian was lost in so many thoughts and questions, trying to fill in as many mental gaps as possible. Hours and hours dragged on, and Aaron's walking became labored. Lucian tried to support Aaron as best as he could, even carrying Aaron on his back for a while.

The longer they traveled, the less Lucian's tensions were. Aerus confidently led the way, Eteria happily clung to Master Felix's arm, and Aaron annoyingly bantered with Lucian. Under different circumstances, traveling together with this group might've been fun, but this period was only the calm before the storm.

Although not visible, a thunderstorm raged in the near distance. There was no lightning, but the *cracks!* and *booms!* of the thunder and the smell of rain and electricity overflowed into the atmosphere. Lucian could feel his head starting to hurt. The feeling of electricity, lack of light, and loud sounds made him jolt. Aaron called him a "scaredy cat," but he was on edge, too.

Looking back at them, Aerus announced, "A thunderstorm is a good sign. It means that we're close to The Court of The Fallen Judge."

"Enna sure likes to put on a show," Master Felix said. "I'm sure that he's thrilled to see me here after all of these years. I should've brought him a gift."

In a half-joking tone, Aerus said, "You brought me as a gift, my friend. Serving a god's soul on a silver platter is sure to entertain him."

Enna? What kind of god's name is Enna?

Forgetting for the umpteenth time that the gods could hear his thoughts, Lucian was startled when Eteria answered his internal question by saying, "The High Judge of The Fallen Realm's full name is Gehenna, my sweet and ignorant Luce. We, ancient gods, love to give nicknames to each other. Let's just say it's an inside joke."

As if they were criminals committing a heist, a flood of lights beamed at them, exposing their positions. After adjusting to the brightness, Lucian quickly took the chance to survey his surroundings. He soon realized that he hadn't missed much of the scenery since there wasn't anything to start with. The land around them was completely barren, devoid of life: no plants, no animals, and no trees.

So, this is what they meant when they said this realm

was a sanctuary for bodiless souls. Even if you had a physical form, you couldn't survive here.

Echoing through the emptiness, an unfamiliar voice announced their arrival. "Welcome to The Court of The Fallen Judge, O sacred souls. Enter my divine abode, and you shall be spared from the elements. Walk through the gates."

Turning around to see the structure, Lucian focused his attention on the gigantic gate rising in front of him. *Impressive* wasn't the right word. The gate was *imposing*. For a structure that didn't seem to be connected to anything, it served as a solid warning that would easily ward away any intruders.

Peering down the brightly lit walkway that stretched past the gate, Lucian saw a structure that seemed twice as large as the gate even from a distance. Rectangular in form and tall, the structure looked different from any building that he had seen in all of Gaia. It also gave off a chilling aura, more terrifying than The Terrasian Palace...

Taking one step past the gate sent him hurdling through time and space. Separated from his friends, apart from Aaron who held tightly onto his back, he fell straight through The Throne Room's ceiling flat onto the floor. Lucian landed so hard on his back that his spine screamed at him. He struggled on his back like an overturned turtle.

Aaron, however, seemed to fare better, as he had used Lucian as a cushion.

Carefully watching their every movement from the sidelines like a predator stalking his prey, the slightly familiar voice spoke again by saying, "Thank you for traveling to The Fallen Realm, Reincarnate of Morpheus, Lucian Roux, and Reincarnate of Adonis, Damian Marlais."

Both Lucian and Aaron simultaneously looked up at the figure, who leisurely sat before them on a throne decorated with branches and thorns. Gehenna, The High Judge of The Fallen Realm, had a creepy expression on his pale face. With neon-green hair and blood-red eyes, he looked like a slimy snake. Sitting sideways on his throne, he lazily asked, "So, which one is it?"

Not thinking before speaking, Lucian asked, "Which one is *what*?"

With an excited sparkle in his eyes, Gehenna said, "The sacrifice, my boy."

21

A DEADLY DEAL

 *The Throne Room*

"Either of your souls will do." Gehenna condescendingly peered down at them. Sitting snugly on his thorny throne, he looked like a dictator. While no crown sat atop his head and no royal cape was wrapped around his neck, he emanated enough authoritative energy to assert his eminence. His snake-like appearance was amplified by his exposed fangs and his braided hair that coiled around his body.

"Neither of us is the sacrifice," Aaron remarked, angrily. "Let us go."

"Ha! How intriguing," Gehenna exclaimed, propping his chin up with his hand and disregarding the boy's words. "Damian, you really *are* the Reincarnate of Adonis.

You two share the same stoic personality. Although, if I didn't know the truth, I would've said that Lucian was Adonis because of the physical similarities."

Damian? Lucian wondered. *Where do I know that name from... Oh, wait! That's the name of the failed Elector-to-be, the one who Master Felix mentioned all of those years ago. But what does that have to do with Aaron? What's going on...*

"Ah, so he didn't explain anything to you, you poor thing," Gehenna said, in a semi-playful, semi-mocking tone. The god seemed to be lost in his own little world until he remembered that he had to finish his explanation. "Aaron Knight's true name is Damian Marlais. Whether a god or a human, everyone seems to love using fake identities. That's the funny part of this entire equation. Isn't Akar supposed to be the liar, or did I miss something?"

"Why are you able to say his name?" Lucian asked, ignoring the god's trite taunts.

A bored look settled on Gehenna's face as he explained, "Oh, you mean how I can say Akar's name while Aerus and Eteria can't? Well, the explanation is a lot simpler than you might imagine. The pact formed between the humans and the gods was limited to the gods of The Heavenly Realm and The Earthly Realm. Since I'm a god of The Fallen Realm, I was one of the only exceptions to the curse.

On top of that, I'm a High Judge. We don't enter pacts lightly."

Struggling to stand, Aaron said, "If you won't take anyone else, then I'll be the sacrifice. That's what you wanted all along, isn't it?"

Gehenna's frown turned upside down into a closed-mouth smile as he said, "Don't be so hasty, hatchling. Why don't we play a game to decide which soul should be sacrificed?"

"What's wrong with you?" Lucian asked in a disgusted tone. "We're not here to play games. We're here to—"

"—retrieve the second heart. Yes, yes, I know, I know. If you really want the second heart, however, then you'll need to do much more than sacrifice one of your souls for it. Decades and decades of utter boredom have driven me completely mad. If you manage to make me laugh, I'll gladly give it to you."

"Lucian, don't listen to him," Aaron coughed out the words along with specks of black blood. "We, no, I don't have much time left. Gehenna is known as a trickster god. We could end up spending centuries trying to make him laugh. We would be better off fighting him for it."

As if he were scolding a child, Gehenna wagged his index finger as he said, "Tsk. Tsk. Tsk. Unlike the previous gods you faced in the past, I'm neither cursed nor weak. You two Reincarnates are certainly stronger than normal humans, but you shouldn't underestimate what it means to declare war against me, The High Judge of The Fallen Realm. Alas, I will applaud you for your audacity, but you will *never* defeat me in a one-to-one battle. Perish the thought."

Ignoring Aaron's warning, Lucian proclaimed, "I'll accept your challenge but only on one condition. If you refuse to comply, then we'll go with Aaron's plan and fight you until either of us dies. I'm not too sure how smoothly our deaths will go over with our friends outside, namely Morpheus and Aerus, however."

"Name your condition," Gehenna responded with a widening grin.

"My condition is simple. Not only will you tell me how to stop Aaron from turning into a Soulless, but you also will let him leave unharmed."

While the delivery of his words was subpar, the weight behind them was properly conveyed to his intended target. Gehenna appeared to be satisfied with the deal, as he summoned a dagger and a chalice out of thin air. He used the dagger to slit the flesh of his palm, drawing bits of blood without even a wince. Bits turned into streams as the blood filled the cup.

With the flick of his finger, the chalice floated toward Lucian's direction. Lucian snatched the cup out of the air and stared at it uneasily. "Drink me," were the words etched into the side of the chalice. Before he could back out of the deal, he plugged his nose and chugged down the blood. While the blood didn't taste as metallic as it should've been, it still burned his throat.

"Lucian, you idiot! What have you done?" Aaron shouted, unsteadily moving toward him. "Blood pacts made with gods are irreversible. If you fail to make him laugh, then you could be stuck here as his jester until the day you die, or worst-case scenario, for all eternity!"

For the first time since they fell into the room, Gehenna rose from his throne. Standing to his full height, Lucian realized that the god standing before them was more intimidating than expected, contrary to his first impression. Gehenna was a monolith at six, no, seven feet tall. He looked like a behemoth snake. Leisurely, he descended the stairs whistling all the way. Even the casual facade that he radiated sent shivers down Lucian's spine.

"You know, I always did get along better with Morpheus than Adonis. That's not just because Morpheus was the protector of the passage between The Earthly Realm and The Fallen Realm, but because he had a more *flexible* mindset. Unlike his boorish brother, who only knew how to sneer in my presence," the god reminisced, fondly. "I like you, Lucian, and I think, by the end of the deal, you'll want to stay with me of your own accord."

"Stop spouting crap!" Aaron screamed. "I told you I'd be the sacrifice. Let Lucian go!"

Gehenna reached the bottom of the staircase and approached Aaron. Playfully, the god flicked Aaron on his forehead, causing him to stumble backward. Losing his balance, Aaron fell flat on his backside. While Aaron glared daggers into the god, Gehenna had an amused look on his face, but he didn't laugh. Much to Lucian's dismay.

"That level of foolery is not enough to make me laugh," Gehenna remarked, reading Lucian's mind. "He does, however, look quite pitiful in that position. Why don't you help him?"

Assisting Aaron, Lucian stated, "Tell me how to cure him, Gehenna."

"Slow down, slow down, the fun's only begun," Gehenna said while teasing him. "Well, I suppose I could throw you a bone, little one. We're going to play a fun word game. I'll say one word, and you'll say the antonym of that word, okay?"

"Fine," Lucian said, resignedly. "Start."

"Boring."

"*Fun.*"

"Sun."

"*Moon.*"

"Night."

"*Day.*"

"Villain."

"*Hero.*"

"Good."

"*Evil.*"

"Bravo, Reincarnate of Morpheus, I knew you wouldn't bore me. Sadly, that was only round one!" Gehenna said. "I'll give you an easy one for round two—Reincarnate of Adonis."

"*Reincarnate of Morpheus,*" Lucian answered.

"The Terras Empire."

"*The Kingdom of Avrith.*"

"What a surprise!" Gehenna said, clapping his hands. "I thought humans hated history, as they always tended to repeat their past mistakes. But you, my boy, have a good grasp of The Earthly Realm."

Feeling a surge of anger welling within, Lucian's patience started wearing scarily thin. His expression grew darker, and his eyes gleamed with a vicious glow. "Get on with it."

"Last one, I promise," Gehenna said, the levity of his words not dying down at all. "Think really, and I mean really, hard about this one—The Tree of Death."

As soon as Lucian answered with the "Tree of Life," the image of Vita's vial surfaced in his mind. *Of course! Why didn't I think of that sooner? How could I be so stupid?*

Fumbling in his cloak's pockets, Lucian pulled out the

sap from The Tree of Life, which was bestowed upon him by the goddess of life, Vita. Before handing the vial to Aaron, Gehenna planted a seed of greed into Lucian's mind by saying, "I forgot to say, but the sap can only save one of you."

"What do you mean?" Lucian asked.

"Well, both of you are cursed, aren't you?" Gehenna said, with a wide smile.

Lucian looked down at the blue spot marking his body. Although Titania's powers had suppressed the curse, it wasn't cured. Aaron looked at Lucian with a startled face while saying, "Y-You used Morpheus's powers, didn't you?"

Grabbing his hair with both hands in frustration, Aaron asked, "What was the point of my training you if you were going to activate the curse anyway?"

Lucian was visibly peeved while saying, "Well, you never explained anything to me until today, so how should I have known?"

While the two of them were bickering, Lucian noticed that Gehenna was giddily watching them. Although frustrated with the situation, Lucian's answer remained the same. Without hesitation, Lucian shoved the vial of sap into Aaron's mouth. Too weak to refuse, Aaron gulped down the sap. Almost instantly, the black, inky tendrils that had taken root in Aaron's body started to recede, eventually fading away to nothing.

"I don't know what to say other than thank you," Aaron said. "Even after everything I put you through, you still…"

"I'm sorry I didn't figure it out sooner," Lucian said.

Interrupting the sentimental mood, Gehenna, forcing his head in between them, said, "It's time for you to fulfill your end of the deal."

"A promise is a promise," Lucian stated.

"At least give him a hint," Aaron interrupted.

Curling his lips upward, the god said, "Since you're bound to be my servant anyway, a little hint or two won't matter. The thing that brings me the most joy is when I see people struggling and suffering. On that note, why don't you fight a dragon for me?"

First, it was a Syras. Then, it was a snake. After that, it was a tree. And now, it's a dragon… What in Gaia's name is wrong with all of these deranged gods?

"I doubt this dragon is stronger than The Magnus Serpens that I defeated in The Wastelands," Lucian stated, confidently. "So, I'm not sure you'll be too amused."

Stroking the strands of his vibrant green braids, Gehenna sighed while saying, "Sometimes, your likeness to Morpheus is a little too uncanny. Why can't you see that it's about the journey and not the destination? You never know what fun things you'll experience on your way to defeating the dragon. Why not give it a try?"

Before Lucian could make a rebuttal, Gehenna snapped his fingers. Out of thin air, a scroll appeared. The scroll floated slowly down until it rested in Lucian's palms. Opening the scroll, Lucian discovered it was a map of The Fallen Realm. Brightly glowing on the upper right-hand side of the map was a marker.

"See, I'm such a gracious god to let you have a chance to retrieve the second heart and the means to make me laugh," Gehenna stated, emphasizing every single word. "You won't have to worry about the darkness of this realm either, since the map will illuminate your way. Also, there's no time limit! The Fallen Realm and The Earthly Realm operate under different time conventions, after all. For example, you could spend a hundred years here with me, but only a year or two would pass up there. Messes with your mortal brain, doesn't it?"

"Whatever you say," Lucian said, half-heartedly. "What is Aaron supposed to do while I'm fighting this dragon?"

"Don't worry," Gehenna said. "I have a separate task for him, but it's nothing too dangerous. I'm a god of my word, so I'll let him leave *after* the deal is done. Besides, the blood pact makes it so that I can't break the deal even if I wanted to."

"Alright, I'm ready to start when you are," Lucian stated, resolutely.

"One more thing that I forgot to mention, Reincarnate of Morpheus. The Fallen Realm is a dangerous region even for the mighty gods of The Heavenly Realm. Make sure that you always stay positive, or else the shadows in this land will try to eat you alive. The creatures of The Fallen Realm feed on negativity, after all."

Gulping down his fears, Lucian braced himself for yet another duel with death. He looked at Aaron, who gave off two conflicting auras: one of gratefulness and the other of annoyance. Tightening his grip on the map, Lucian nodded his head and signaled the start of the deadly deal.

A final snap of the god's fingers sent Lucian hurdling through time and space again. The fluids in his stomach sloshed back and forth and then up and down. He felt like vomiting. Gehenna's map pulled him through the tunnel and guided him to the starting line.

Tugged through the exit of the tunnel, Lucian landed in a swamp of sorts at the edge of The Fallen Realm, according to the marker on the map. Not only was the dragon's real-time position marked on the map, but Lucian's was as well. Almost a little too fascinated with the magic behind it, he watched his marker move with each step that he took. Forward and backward and side to side, he played around for a bit, until he snapped himself out of it.

I'm acting just like a jester... Has Gehenna laughed yet?

Brighter than the lantern but darker than an illumination crystal, the blue-hued streams pouring out of the map served as his only light source. Peering out into the distance, the swampy surface seemed to extend into eternity. Step by step, his shoes squished against the mud, if that really was the substance beneath him. The further he walked, the faster his stamina drained.

Like the journey to Gehenna's court, the hours passed by slowly. After a while, the weather slightly changed, as the stale and cold air turned hot and humid. Walking forward with his nose to the map, his forehead smacked right into a hard surface. He faltered backward, and his head pounded with pain. It took him a while to realize that the surface he had run headfirst into was a solid yet see-through wall. Beyond the wall was a sea of fog swirling around in the dark abyss. Even with the light source from the map, he couldn't tell what lay deeper within.

Holding up the map, his eyes searched for anything that resembled the area where he was at. Almost as if the map could read his mind, one marker lit up brighter than the rest. Right in between where he started his quest and where the dragon's lair was located, there was an area labeled with swirls and squiggles.

In a fancy font, three words were written in the center of the area: *Sea of Dreams.*

22

REMEMBER THE FALLEN

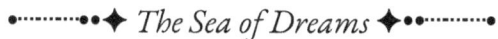 *The Sea of Dreams*

The Sea of Dreams lay behind the invisible barrier. Slashing with his sword, kicking with his feet, and punching with his fists, nothing seemed to work. Each attack further sapped his energy. Fatigue started making its way into his mind, but as Lucian was as stubborn as a mule, he refused to stop.

Replaying the deal with the devil, Lucian remembered the fine print: All he had to do was make the trickster of a god laugh only once. Stopping his barrage of attacks, he lowered himself to the muddy surface, where he sat on his knees and stared at the barrier. Peering into the fog, an idea came to mind, as he meditated. Drawing in a long breath that inflated his lungs until they felt like they were about to burst, he calmed and braced himself.

In a strong upward swing of his neck, he released all of the stored air from his lungs into the atmosphere and yelled several octaves higher than normal, "DID YOU HEAR ABOUT THE MAN WHO TRIED TO CATCH FOG?"

Letting the ensuing silence linger, he then answered his own pun:

"HE MIST!"

After finishing the fool's pun, his face flushed a bright red. Never in his life would he have imagined trying to use the joke that he had learned from Barren in *this* situation and under *these* conditions. A single tear started to form in his right eye as he lamented his foolishness.

Standing up, Lucian approached the foggy barrier once more. He reached out to touch it, hoping that Gehenna was entertained enough to let him in. Luckily for him, the rock-solid wall turned mellow like a marshmallow, and he slipped into the Sea of Dreams. Not knowing who heard him, he kept slapping his face to snap himself out of his humiliation. Being a laughingstock was nothing new for him, but he refused to be ridiculed by a god.

Somewhere deep within the fog, he saw a clearing of sorts: a place where the fog fully dispersed and where he saw two signs wedged snugly in the mud. One of them read, *Head right to reach The Dragon's Lair.* The other one of them read: *Head left to walk down memory lane.*

Not in the mood for games, he decided to do the smart thing and check the map. Unfortunately, his personal marker kept spinning every which way as if there was some sort of magical interference. Not too shocked by this impediment, he headed to the right, as the sign said. For some reason, however, he ended up back in the same space.

The two signs seemed to mock him silently. No matter which way he chose, he always ended up back at the two signs. Frustration bred negativity, and out of the swamp came the creatures. Small, spiky black creatures emerged, grabbing at him and clinging to his clothes. He shook them off, but they stuck to him like gum. That was when he remembered Gehenna's warning.

Think positive thoughts, Lucian internally recited. *I'm fine. Everything's fine. I'm going to solve this problem and then find the correct path. Breathe in and breathe out, Lucian.*

Changing his way of thinking, the spiky creatures detached from him and slinked back into the swamp. Creepy as they were, he had a strong desire to never see them again. Going back to the problem at hand, he walked around to see the backside of the signs. Two separate messages were written, "In the Sea of Dreams, there is something you must find" and "Say my name, and I shall be your guide."

Without taking too much time to think, he simply started saying every name that came to mind. Every name from Gehenna to Angelique came out of his mouth until he landed on one name, Eteria. A shrill squeal echoed throughout the entire area, and he shuddered at the thought of her appearing out of nowhere.

With an annoyingly loud voice, she announced, "Welcome to the Sea of Dreams, little Luce! Are you ready to walk down memory lane? Everything from your first baby steps to your deepest darkest secrets will be uncovered, so make sure that your heart and soul are prepared for this magical trip through time. Once you're ready, please head in a straight line forward!"

Resigned to his fate, he walked straight forward through the fog. After a few steps, he saw the shadowy figures of his mother, Lucille, and himself, as a newborn baby, hovering above the waters. Not having any childhood photos, he felt both longing and sadness.

"Lucian Roux, during the height of spring, was born to Lucille Roux, the Crown Princess of Lunaris," Eteria said as smoothly as if she were reading a script. "The 25-year-old Lucille was ecstatic to have such a healthy bouncing baby boy, and so was his father, Remus Roux."

Seeing the sign hopping up and down in a comical

fashion made him want to punch it with all of his might. He refrained from doing so, as he didn't want to breed any negativity that would cause the spiky creatures to resurface. That last part, however, stuck strangely in his mind: Lucian's mother was the Crown Princess of Lunaris. Although he thought this revelation to be a joke at first, it *did* shed light on Eva's explanation back in Terras. Akar had stolen children from royalty and nobility, and those children seemed to have stronger connections to the ancient gods. If he truly was of a royal bloodline, then it would make some sense why he was able to store Morpheus's soul, unlike the rest of the Reincarnates.

Then, Lucian remembered how Aaron's face looked when Lucian made that stupid joke, asking, "Who died and made you king?"

They're just trying to trick me and rile me up. Stop thinking about stupid things.

Every few feet, more signs popped up, and Eteria explained every single one. Just as Aaron had mentioned, there were many things from his past that he didn't remember, no matter how hard he tried. Lucian couldn't remember how his mother died, when his father married Melinda, or why he forgot about Aaron and Seraphina. The cutouts clearly showed the three of them playing as children.

He couldn't help but agonize over the discrepancies in

his memories. There were only two scenarios that could reasonably explain his memory loss: First, Aaron was lying to him, and these images were meant to mess with him. Second, Aaron was telling him the truth, and Akar had altered his memories. Either way, his fretting was causing him to panic, so he desperately tried to stop. The heads of the spiky creatures reared their ugly heads at the water's surface, so Lucian forced a smile, hoping to replicate a happy state.

The final shadowy figure was a replica of his current self. Staring into the hollow, black eyes, Lucian shuddered. When Lucian was a foot or so away, the shadowy figure started to float in a certain direction. It led him to another clearing in the fog, where there were no signs. Eteria had also ceased with her announcements.

As soon as Lucian stepped into the clearing, he was sucked down into the swampy surface. Plugging his nose, closing his eyes, and filling his lungs with air, he allowed the mud to engulf him. Entering the other side, he emerged, flipping about like a fish.

Once he caught his breath, he realized the scenery around him had drastically shifted. Instead of the foggy and swampy area, the village of Caelum appeared before him.

"Remember," a voice as soft as a whisper said, "Don't be deceived. Everything in the Sea of Dreams is nothing more than a fantasy. Remember from whence you came. Remember..."

The voice faded away.

Stretching out before him was a gorgeous scene. Rolling hills and running rivers filled his view. Besides the beauty of the land, wafts of delicious food filled his nostrils. His stomach gurgled at the smell, and his nose led him back to his house.

Snapping himself out of his trance for a split second, the drunken image of his father flashed into his head. Just as fast as the fear came, it quickly left him. He drifted into his house almost like he was a feather floating in the air.

"Lucian, the bread is almost fully baked," a loving voice said. "I bet your father is hungry since he met with the Elders earlier, so I cooked something delicious. Want to try a piece?"

Tears welled in his eyes at the sight of his mother, who was alive and standing right in front of him. He nodded his head in response multiple times and ran to her side. Nuzzling his face into her cooking apron, he felt safe. Just as safe as he had been when he was a child.

Remembering what the ominous voice said before returning home, he stopped in his tracks. The smell of the baked bread, however, appealed to his stomach so much that it overloaded his brain. He couldn't think straight. His mouth watered profusely at the mere sniff of food. Breaking off a piece of the loaf, his mother fed it to him.

After swallowing a small piece, he felt tired.

Too tired.

Fighting against his instincts, he tried to break the spell. Running to the front door, he slammed right into his father, Remus. Even though it was an accident, even the slightest physical contact with his father sent him flying backward. Lucian broke out into a cold sweat. Flashbacks to his father's violence and abuse made him nauseous.

Lucian's vision narrowed, and his heart raced. How could he escape when the man who made his life miserable stood in his way? While Lucille and Remus were speaking, his father noticed something strange about Lucian's behavior. Walking toward him, his father reached out his hand to touch him. Lucian retreated further backward, reliving every repressed fear that he had tried helplessly to forget.

Years of suffering weren't so easy to get rid of, after all. Remus was a villain as evil as the Akar in his nightmares. Lucian's mind was a jumbled mess, so he couldn't rely on his rationale to save him. His instincts needed to guide him. His muscles were tensed, as his body was expected to fight. However, his father didn't attack him. Instead, Remus hugged him.

"Hey, kiddo," Remus said, in a sickeningly sweet tone, stroking the back of Lucian's head. "Don't you remember when we used to play hero and villain when you were small? You're a little too old for make-believe, but I'll tell you what. Whatever you're struggling with now, just remember that your mother and I will always love you, no matter what."

Streams of tears trickled down Lucian's face. He sobbed loudly for the first time in forever. Like a little child, he let his emotions overflow. He waited years and years for his father to return to his loving self, but his wish was never granted.

And sadly, it never would be granted. Not now, not ever.

Releasing his father and wiping away his tears, Lucian asked, "Are you satisfied, Gehenna? Have I suffered enough for you yet? I bet this touching scene really makes you laugh, right? Don't tell me that you seriously expected me to believe that my distant and delusional father would ever recover and say those sappy words to me. I know what you're planning to do. Well, let me tell you it won't work on me, you hear me? Both my mother and my father are *dead*. Stop using them to try to manipulate me."

Although there was no verbal response, the scene abruptly changed again. The house disintegrated into nothingness, and the faces of his mother and his father faded too. Hearing a sound like the drop of water on a still lake, Lucian stood in a realm where there was a cloudless sky and clear blue water beneath him. The rightful owner of the voice that always would say, "*YOU MUST CHOOSE*," now had a name and a face.

The High Judge of The Heavenly Realm floated several inches above the water, staring straight into Lucian's soul. With six small wings extending from his back and a pure-white gown flowing like waves to the ground, he emitted an almighty, regal aura. Unlike Gehenna, who slithered the surface like a snake, this Judge soared the skies like an eagle.

"Tell me thy name, child of Gaia."

Not sure whether to bow or to kneel, Lucian remained upright and said, "My name is Lucian Roux, and I am the Reincarnate of Morpheus, the god of destruction."

"I am Veritas, the god who governs The Heavenly Realm," The High Judge stated. "The Heavenly Realm and The Fallen Realm are like two sides of the same coin, with Gaia serving as the center. What befalls Gaia affects all of us. You, the child of Gaia, will finally have the chance to choose your own fate."

"Are you trying to mock me? Isn't this entire scene an illusion created by Gehenna?" Lucian asked, cautiously yet seriously. "I don't have time for these stupid games, Gehenna. I need to retrieve the second heart to defeat Akar and save Gaia! To hell with your amusement!"

Landing on the surface of the water, Veritas said, "I am

not Gehenna, child of Gaia. While my physical form cannot travel to The Fallen Realm, I *can* send my spirit here for short periods of time. What you are seeing now is *no* illusion. But alas, I suppose actions speak louder than words."

Floating toward him, Veritas tapped Lucian's chest with his right index finger. A warmth blossomed near Lucian's heart, and it spread throughout his body—from the strands of his hair to the tips of his toes. What felt like an enormous weight lifted from him.

"What did you do?"

"In exchange for purifying the curse from Morpheus's soul," Veritas said, "I need you to do something for me."

"What is it?"

"As you may know, The High Judges aren't allowed to interfere with the affairs of the other realms. I have heard of the suffering of my fellow gods and goddesses, cursed and trapped in The Earthly Realm," Veritas explained. "Since you shall inevitably fight against Akar, my request is simple: Form a blood pact with me. When Akar's soul is split from his bodily vessel, say my name, so that I may know when it is time to act. Use the second heart to open the gate to The Heavenly Realm and send him to me. As a former god of The Heavenly Realm, Akar's soul shall be punished under my jurisdiction."

"Why should I trust you?"

"A blood pact is eternal. Even if you perish, the pact will stay in effect. We gods are bound by our souls and by our words."

"I must admit that forming two blood pacts wasn't how I expected my day to go, but I suppose it's not a bad thing," Lucian said. "But you still haven't explained how I'm supposed to separate Akar's soul from his bodily vessel."

"Can you not critically think for yourself, or must I lay out everything at your feet?"

Without a shred of hesitation or shame, Lucian responded, "At my feet, please."

Letting out a long sigh, Veritas stated, "Fine, I suppose you deserve an explanation. To separate a foreign soul from a bodily vessel, you must force the vessel's original owner to regain his sense of self. The stronger the shock, the better the result. This is the way that souls work."

Awaken Elias's soul? No way! Is that the lesser of the two evils?

Still reeling from Veritas's response, Lucian proceeded with yet another unresolved question and asked, "I've answered your cryptic question time and time again, so what exactly are you trying to make me choose?"

Tapping Lucian's forehead, Veritas sent a flurry of painful memories and destructive visions directly into his thoughts. From the destruction of The Three Realms to the death of every life form in existence, not a single soul was to be spared. Under the rule of Akar, the realms would be reduced to desolation and destruction. Lucian's choice, then, was to either let the realms fall into ruin or to save them.

Disrupting Lucian's internal debate, Veritas asked, "So, shall we form the pact or not?"

Reluctantly, Lucian nodded his head, repeating the same process with Veritas as with Gehenna. He drank the blood, and the liquid embedded itself deep into his soul. Bound to the pact, Lucian was released back into the Sea of Dreams in The Fallen Realm. Although he didn't defeat a dragon, he gained an invaluable pact in the process. Once again, the muddy waters of the swamp were sloshing under his feet.

A booming voice echoed throughout the land. This time, however, the voice's owner wasn't Eteria. It was Gehenna himself. "Curse you, Veritas!" Gehenna roared aloud. "Don't think you'll get away with ruining my fun, you boorish god!"

As loud as lightning, a snap and a crackle transported Lucian back into The Throne Room. Aaron and Gehenna awaited him. Scoping out the scene from above, Lucian noticed Aaron's annoyed look and Gehenna's enraged expression. As soon as Lucian landed on the marble floor, Gehenna gripped his shoulders in anger and shook him so hard that he felt vomit traveling up his throat.

"What did that pompous god say to you?" Gehenna said while tightening his iron grip. "Tell me everything, and don't you dare leave out a single detail. I need to know, now!"

Prying Gehenna's hands off Lucian's shoulders, Aaron intervened and said, "Let him go, Gehenna. Lucian has already fulfilled his end of the deal."

"What do you mean?" Lucian asked.

Rubbing his temples, Aaron explained, "This foolish god laughed the moment that you hit your head against the wall of the barrier. He extended your suffering for his own amusement. Your encounter with the god, Veritas, was neither an illusion nor a plan. So, are you ready?"

"Ready for what?" Lucian asked, knowing very well the answer to Aaron's question.

"Ready to defeat Akar?"

23

THEY WILL RISE AGAIN

"Y**ou shall not pass!**" Gehenna blocked the exit. Aaron walked past him. Lucian followed suit. "B-B-But you didn't defeat the dragon!" Gehenna said, throwing a god-sized tantrum. "We didn't even finish our game."

Looking behind him, Lucian said, in a matter-of-fact tone, "The deal is done, Gehenna. We won. Screw your game."

Doing the same as Lucian, Aaron said, "Besides, we *did* defeat the dragon, since we defeated *you*."

Gasping dramatically, Gehenna asked, "How did you know the dragon was *me*?"

"You're not as sly as you think you are," Aaron stated.

"Besides, only an infant wouldn't make the connection that you, Gehenna, are the ancient dragon of The Fallen Realm. You look and act like a lazy lizard. Dragons are undeniably characterized by their greed and their need for entertainment."

Guess, I'm an infant, Lucian lamented.

"Don't think you can leave without..." Gehenna started to say, desperately grasping for something around his neck, "...This!"

Brimming with confidence, Gehenna held a plain old rock tied together by a string in his hand. Just like a lizard, his face started turning green with scales forming on his skin. He looked more and more like a dragon as he realized he had been tricked.

Aaron had a nasty smirk on his face, watching the ancient god grow angrier with glee. Lucian remembered why it was a good thing Aaron wasn't his enemy anymore. Showing off the stolen blue gemstone wrapped around his neck, Aaron said, "Isn't it ironic? That the trickster got played at his own game?"

"Aaron, that's enough," Lucian said, realizing that the ancient god was reaching a boiling point. "Let's not escalate things."

A wicked smile flashed on his face as Aaron said, "Back off, Lucian. Let me take revenge on this slimy snake."

Assuming a condescending stance and look, Gehenna

cackled while saying, "Revenge? All I did was make you feed my precious snakes. You never said that you were afraid."

Reaching for his Phantom sword, Aaron grasped at an empty hilt. An expression of absolute horror crossed his face as he looked at Lucian and asked, "Where's my sword, Lucian?"

Playing the fool, Lucian shrugged while saying, "Hmm, I'm not exactly sure. Maybe it's taking a nice nap back in Caelum?"

"I *need* my sword, Lucian!" Aaron seethed, wildly waving his hands in the air.

"Don't worry, Barren can always make you a new one," Lucian said, laxly. "No need to throw a fit."

Trying to form a coherent sentence, Aaron stated, "Oh, I see. Then, why don't I throw your sword into the swamp of The Fallen Realm and see how you fare without him?"

"I'd like to see you try."

Just as Aaron was about to pull Lucian's hair from his head, Master Felix appeared alongside Aerus, Eteria, and Seraphina.

"I have a lot of things I'd like to say to you two, but we don't have time," Master Felix said. "First, Aaron, how would Lucian have known that Phantom wasn't just a sword if you didn't tell him? Second, Lucian, try to show a little compassion. You're better than this childish bickering."

Lucian apologized.

Aaron apologized afterward.

"So, what?" Lucian said, as he finally realized the truth about Phantom. "Phantom is the same as Ignis?"

"Of course, he is, you imbecile," Aaron stated. "Why do you think I worked so hard to retrieve him from the armory in Caelum?"

Scratching his head, Lucian admitted, "I simply thought that you were obsessed with swords."

Forcibly diverting the conversation, Master Felix said, "Alright, that's enough, you two. Remember the prophetic words? You need two hearts to act together to defeat the evil one. Pick your battles wisely, or else you'll lose all of them."

Eteria and Aerus nodded in agreement with Master Felix's words of wisdom.

Seraphina approached Lucian and Aaron. Her eyes momentarily met with Master Felix's, who simply nodded his head. She grabbed their hands, pulled them close, and said, "I think it's time that I told you two the truth."

"The truth?" Lucian and Aaron asked in unison.

Shaking like a leaf, she said, "As you know, the prophecy foretells of a person who can manipulate memories. Well, that someone is *me*. Even if I was under Akar's influence, I was the one who erased not only Lucian's but also Aaron's memories. I'm so sorry. None of this would've happened if I had broken free from his control sooner. Perhaps if I had been braver, Lucian would've been spared from his father's abuse, and Aaron wouldn't have been abandoned in The Terras Empire."

"W-What are you talking about?" Lucian let the words spill out of his mouth like a waterfall. "I don't understand what you're trying to say. How is my father's abuse your fault? What memories exactly did you erase?"

"Every memory related to your mother, Lucille Roux, from the minds of those she loved and who loved her in return," she explained, sullenly. "Lucian, what exactly do you remember regarding your mother's death?"

He ran through all of his memories related to his mother. However, none of them were related to her death. Not only could he not recall the *how*, but he also couldn't recall the *why* behind her demise. He couldn't contain his confusion and started rambling to himself.

Seraphina continued her explanation by saying, "I'm sorry that I didn't come forward with this sooner... I didn't want either of you to hate me. I'm so sorry for my selfish behavior. You must know, though, that Lucille asked me to keep the reason behind her death a secret because she didn't want either of you to bear the burden of her death. She told me to reveal these secrets to you only when you were ready to learn the truth and defeat Akar."

Lucian couldn't believe what he was hearing, so he asked, "So, you're saying that my entire life was a lie? Did my father know the truth, too?"

"Your life is *not* a lie, Lucian," she refuted. "At least, not to me. In regard to your other question, the answer is *no*. Akar commanded me to rewrite your father's memory regarding your mother's death as well."

"I still don't understand, Seraphina. Why would Akar need to resort to such extremes? Wasn't Lucian's mother a normal human being? What could've caused her to make Akar feel *that* threatened? So far as to erase my memories too?" Aaron asked.

"Piecing together the conversations that I overheard from Akar and Lucille," Seraphina explained, "I believe that she found out about The Harvesting and tried to stop him from molding you both into his vessel. As for why Akar felt threatened, I think it was because Lucille was a powerful person capable of piercing through his illusions and lies. She was so powerful that even my abilities couldn't erase her memories. The only way to stop her from escaping with the two of you was for Akar to kill her."

Akar killed my mother...?

Trying to come to terms with what he heard and trying

to figure out Aaron's involvement, Lucian asked, "What about Aaron? What's his role in this whole scenario?"

"Before Akar confronted her, Lucille spoke to Aaron's mother, Silvia, and advised her to escape with Aaron during the night of The Winter Solstice. For whatever reason, the barrier surrounding Caelum would always weaken in the winter season, so they should've been able to escape safely without alerting a single soul. The four of them were supposed to leave together, but Lucille's plans were derailed when she was suddenly summoned with her whole family to The Sanctuary of Gaia, where Akar detained her."

"If Aaron escaped, how was his memory erased?"

"It's because we didn't, Lucian," Aaron answered. "We failed."

"You're correct," Seraphina confirmed. "Akar was no fool. He suspected the escape plan and captured Aaron and his mother before they crossed the barrier. Once Akar deemed Aaron a failed vessel, they were banished from the village, while you and Remus were demoted to a lower district."

Seraphina broke out into a sob, releasing the shame that she had been suffering with for so long. While a rage was rising within Lucian's heart, he subdued an outburst for her sake. Wrapping his arms around her, Lucian said, "It's not your fault, Seraphina. Don't blame yourself. It wasn't you who killed her. It was *him*. Thank you for telling me the truth about my mother. I suppose the greatest sacrifices truly are the ones that are done out of love."

"After that day, I vowed in my heart to help you in any way that I could," Seraphina said, slowly regaining her composure. "I'm not sure if my powers will work directly on Akar, but I do know that they work on everyone else. I'm assuming that Akar will use every trick in the book, including using your sister as his hostage. With my abilities, I can rewrite and restore her memories to the way they were before."

"What do you mean?" Lucian asked. "Why would you need to restore her memories? I saw her at the palace. She wasn't missing any memories."

"Not the memories about you," Seraphina explained. "The memories about what Akar made her do. The attack on your family was orchestrated by Akar, Lucian. He placed the blame on Aaron to hide the fact that he had kidnapped Rosalie."

"Why would Akar go to so much trouble to trick her and to trick us?" Lucian asked. "Rosalie isn't even a Reincarnate."

"Rosalie *is* a Reincarnate, Lucian," Seraphina revealed. "Not just any Reincarnate, but she's the one-and-only goddess of hypnosis, Fantasia. Rosalie's disappearance was no mystery. Under Akar's orders, she was dispatched to The Terras Empire to sway public opinion. With her powers, she was able to place Elias as a puppet ruler on The Terrasian Throne."

"But why would she so willingly follow along with Akar's plan?" Lucian asked. "I understand some of my memories are missing, but to believe that Rosalie has been a Reincarnate this entire time is ridiculous."

Shaking her head, Seraphina said, "I too was trapped under Akar's curse. Only once my curse was suppressed, thanks to Felix, Aerus, and Eteria, was I finally free to speak my mind and tell you the truth. In Rosalie's case, ever since Akar discovered that Melinda was a spy working for ATF, he continuously threatened to expose and kill her mother if Rosalie didn't comply with his commands. As punishment, I had to erase portions of Rosalie's memories about her childhood, her mother, and you."

"If that's true, then I can't fight her..."

"I know," she said. "That's why I'll fight her in your stead. As we share similar strengths, it'll be an equal playing field. At the same time, I'll try to restore her memories. You need only to defeat Akar. When he's been vanquished, the realms and the gods should return to normal."

"And if they don't return to normal?" Lucian asked, his fingers twisting into a fist and knuckles whitening under the exerted pressure. "What will happen to her, then?"

Seraphina's torn expression foretold the future more clearly than any words could.

Lucian braced himself for the battle to come—a battle that he couldn't afford to lose, no matter the cost. To make amends, Seraphina restored the missing pieces of his memory. Everything from his first day of school to his first fight with Aaron-as-Damian returned to him. The weight of the world seemed to fall on his shoulders.

Aaron rested his hand on Lucian's right shoulder as he said, "Remember, the two hearts acting as one are necessary to win this war. You're not alone, Lucian. We're all here to help you: Felix, Aerus, Eteria, Ignis, Seraphina, and me."

"I suppose you're right," Lucian admitted. "I never was the type to mull things over."

"So, we're all set, right?" Aaron asked. "We have our hearts, our warriors, and our weapons. Well, we'll have our weapons once we reach Caelum, thanks to someone forgetting to grab my sword."

Let it go already, you sword-loving freak.

"You're missing a fundamental piece of the equation," Lucian stated. "How are we supposed to return to the surface? It's not like there are any flying monkeys that we can ride to return to The Earthly Realm.

Looking over at Gehenna, Lucian asked, "Wait...is there?"

Shaking his head, Gehenna stated, "Not flying monkeys, but a powerful dragon is sitting right in front of you."

"Why, we are so blessed, O great and mighty god," Aaron said, in a sarcastic tone. "So, what's the catch?"

"No catch," Gehenna said. "Let's just say that Akar is a thorn in my side."

Looking at the trio of gods, Lucian asked, "What about Master Felix, Aerus, and Eteria?"

"Don't worry about us, Lucian," Master Felix reassuringly said. "Once you're in The Earthly Realm, we'll return to our rightful places by your side."

Without warning, Gehenna transformed into his dragon form. The small scales that were shown previously were nothing compared with their true size. A long tail sprouted from his lower backside, and his full form extended to extreme lengths and heights. Truly, if nothing else, Gehenna was an awe-inspiring creature of legend. Even if he had an ego.

Swooping the three of them onto his back, Gehenna burst through The Throne Room's ceiling and ascended to the upper section of The Fallen Realm. Looking from above to down below, Lucian noticed that the fog and the darkness spread for miles and miles to the farthest regions of the realm. He couldn't even believe that he had ventured alone into such a mysterious area, even with a map.

Approaching the boundary between The Fallen Realm and The Earthly Realm, Gehenna said one last thing, "You're on your own from here on out. Remember to come to visit me again, as I have many more spectacular games that we can play together."

Breaking off from the dragon's main body, three scales lifted them upward through the boundary. The scales that they each sat on were surprisingly sturdy and floated upward on their own accord. Each of their souls shook in their bodies as they left the realm.

Upon breaking through the barrier between realms, the three scales evaporated, and a gloomy sky greeted them. The passengers landed safely on the dirt. Out of the dark fog, two figures appeared before them: Akar and Rosalie.

With a sinister-sounding voice, the taller figure said, "Welcome home, my rebellious vessel and his party of rebels. I see you've safely returned from your journey to The Fallen Realm. With Gehenna's erratic personality, I was worried that you wouldn't return to me in time for the ceremony."

Akar-as-Elias walked toward them with Rosalie by his side. Lucian instantly noticed that Rosalie was acting weird. She had hollow, silver stones for eyes that looked as if they were staring into the abyss. He tried shaking off the creepiness of her stare... The more that he looked, the sicker he felt.

Placing his arm around her shoulder, Akar stated, "Isn't she such a *doll*? At first, I didn't think I could easily control her until I happened to mention that her precious older brother abandoned her for good. All it took was a little lie."

Every emotion that Lucian could muster rose to the surface, calling him to action. "What have you done to my sister, you disgusting piece of—"

"—I wouldn't finish that sentence if I were you," Akar said, teasingly. "Your sister can still hear you, my misguided vessel. You wouldn't want to make yourself look more like a disappointment than you already are, do you?"

Impulsively reaching for his sword, Lucian lunged at him.

Aaron pulled Lucian back by his collar, while Seraphina latched onto Lucian's arm.

"Stop falling for the same tricks," Aaron reprimanded. "He's trying to upset you."

"Aaron's right," Seraphina agreed. "We need to avoid doing anything rash since he has control over your sister."

"Always the smart cookies, these two," Akar said. "Lucian, you could learn a thing or two from your friends. You wouldn't want to lose more of your loved ones because of one bad decision. Oh, that reminds me of the time when you left the villagers to die."

Regaining his composure, Lucian said, "I'll make you eat those words, Akar. Don't forget that we're the ones with the upper hand, not you."

"Do you really believe that you can defeat a god simply because you have those stupid stones? Think again! I didn't spend centuries crafting this plan for mere mortals to stand in my way."

With a cheeky smile on his face and a defiant gleam in his eyes, Aaron stated, "Say that *after* you've defeated us, Akar. We'll show you just how strong mere mortals can be."

Weapons at the ready, the trio waged war against the ancient god of deception, Akar.

24
RETURN OF THE RISEN

 *Caelum*

As soon as the fight started, Seraphina signaled to Lucian and Aaron that she was ready to start the plan. Diverting Rosalie's attention with offensive spells, the two of them disappeared into the fog. With Rosalie out of the picture, Lucian and Aaron could focus on Akar. Or, at least, they were supposed to, but the evil god took his merry time to move or speak. The longer they waited, the more antsy they became.

Reading their minds while casually juggling his scepter, Akar said, "Your measly one-day-old plan can't stop my millennia-old one."

"Stop playing games with us, Akar," Aaron said. "You're only wasting our time."

"You're a lot more on edge than usual," Akar said, reaching for the sword near his waist. "Is it perhaps because of *this*?"

In his right hand, he held his scepter. In his left hand, he held Aaron's sword, Phantom. Aaron looked like he was about to blow a fuse. Like minutes before, but now reversed, Lucian stopped Aaron from leaping out to attack.

"Wait, Aaron," Lucian said, as calmly as he could. "Don't be impulsive."

"Shut up, Lucian," Aaron said. "To win this war, we have to—"

"—Sync the two hearts, I know."

"Are you two lovebirds finished fighting yet?" Akar asked, pointing his scepter at them. "If so, I'd like to see you act out your plan."

"Focus, Aaron," Lucian said. "You don't have your sword, so cover my side."

Nodding their heads at each other, the fight began in a flash. Lucian pulled Ignis out of his sheath, and he ran toward Akar. He held the sword so tight that the hilt's pattern engraved an impression on his palm. In the background, Aaron summoned several Lychnuses of greater size than the one Lucian had fought in Orsus. At their master's command, they raced forward at full speed. Their eyes were trained on Akar, and their feet dredged up dirt as they sprinted. In mere moments, Aaron's Summons appeared at Lucian's side.

Upon spanning the distance between the enemy and himself, Lucian plunged his blade at Akar. Effortlessly, Akar blocked Lucian's attack. The *clash* of sword hitting sword reverberated throughout the dry air. As they continued to fight, Lucian noticed Ignis and Phantom resonating with one another. Like their masters, Ignis and Phantom were like twin swords, as all of their attacks were neutralized by each other. Luckily, Lucian had the Lychnuses to support him and distract Akar's attention, but that tactic didn't last long.

Visibly annoyed with the Lychnus' attacks, Akar, with a single swing of his scepter, cast a spell that spewed out dark energy and tore the Summons to shreds. Aaron let out a painful cry. Lucian reacted to Aaron's reaction, but in the split second that Lucian lost focus, Akar summoned a dust storm that swept him skyward. In the few seconds that Lucian flailed in the air, he caught a glimpse of Aaron's face. He had a look of inexpressible pain.

Then, with another flick of his scepter, Akar pummeled Lucian to the ground.

"What did you think would happen, Damian?" Akar asked, condescendingly. "You're a failure, who can't even use your god's powers—a Summoner, who loses his life force with each summon. A useless thing like you should just die."

Holding his scepter high, Akar gathered the surrounding dirt and rocks, forming a gigantic boulder above his head. Consumed with confidence, Akar's expression warped into a wicked smile. He then swung the scepter down, watching as the boulder descended on Aaron.

Lucian leaped straight into the boulder's path, acting as a blockade between the boulder and Aaron. The boulder smashed right into Lucian's back, but Aerus's protective barrier lessened the blow. However, the impact was so strong that Lucian fell forward, landing on his hands and knees. Chunks of rock rained around them. Thankfully, since Lucian had shielded Aaron with his body, he was mostly unscathed.

Trying to stay focused, Lucian regained his footing. He assumed an offensive form, conjuring the red-and-blue flames from his sword. Like the last time with Elias, Akar extinguished Ignis's flames with ease. Unlike the last time, however, Lucian wasn't fighting alone anymore. From the depth of Lucian's soul, Morpheus's soul awakened. He readily lent Lucian his strength, and his all-consuming black flames replaced Lucian's red-and-blue ones.

With Ignis poised to strike, Lucian ran straight forward. Mid-way to Akar, Lucian made a running jump and swung the flaming sword down at Akar. Making contact with Akar's imperial robe, the black flames greedily ate away at every piece of clothing that they could consume. Hastily throwing off the burning clothes, Akar used his scepter to open a portal, stripped off his robe, and discarded it into a different dimension.

From the heat of the flames, sweat formed on the god's forehead. Every swing of his scepter and sword became more and more defensive. Although Akar seemed to be on the back foot, he consistently dodged all of Lucian's incoming attacks, not giving him another chance.

With a wispy tone, Akar said, "While it looks like you've managed to cure my curse, you are and forever will be a monster."

In between swings, Lucian shouted, "Shut up!"

The longer they fought, the faster Akar adapted to Lucian's attacks. None of Lucian's slashes landed after that first attack, and his stamina drained at an alarming rate. Whether it was pure anger or the desire to protect his friends that fueled him, he didn't know. What he did know, however, was that his strength wouldn't last forever.

In a condescending tone, Akar asked, "Are you so ignorant that you don't realize you're dying? Haven't you ever wondered why Morpheus only grants you a portion of his power?"

Along with Lucian's rising emotions, Morpheus's

black flames strengthened in intensity. "I don't know what you're talking about," Lucian denied. "No matter what lies you spew, there's only one truth…. That I'll defeat you and set everyone free."

Casting a powerful spell, Akar pushed Lucian back to where Aaron was restoring his strength. As soon as Lucian analyzed his friend's condition and the flow of the fight, he knew the tides weren't in their favor. Aaron was exhausted from endlessly summoning the Lychnuses. Lucian, on the other hand, felt his legs turn to lead with each step.

What's happening to me?

"I'll answer that question for you," Akar stated, tapping his chest with his scepter. "Every time that Morpheus interferes with this world, his power eats away at your soul, Lucian. That's why you shouldn't be too hasty to rely on *his* powers."

"Stop spouting lies!"

Grabbing Lucian's shoulder to stop him from attacking again with the black flames, Aaron whispered, in between breaths, "As much as I hate to admit it, Akar's right. It's the other reason why I refuse to use Adonis's powers. Because they broke the pact, manifesting their powers in The Earthly Realm will deteriorate our souls."

"How *are* we supposed to defeat him, then?" Lucian impatiently asked. "The stone hearts are our trump card, but we can't even activate them until we've separated Akar's soul from Elias's body."

"Think of a way," Aaron said. "You know Elias better than I do. Isn't there *some* way that you can wake him up from his beauty sleep?"

Every detail about Elias ran through Lucian's head. From The Rebirth Festivals to the Parsley Twins, he tried as hard as he could to piece together a plan to force Elias to resurface. The only things and people that Lucian knew Elias loved were his pride, his power, his object of obsession, Emilia, and his porky minions, the Parsley Twins.

"Pride plus power equals..." Lucian calculated, "*Ego.*"

Before Lucian could finish thinking, Akar unleashed another series of elemental spells. Using wind, water, fire, and earth, all kinds of attacks flew at Lucian. Although Lucian managed to fend them off, he found it nearly impossible to span the gap between him and Akar again. Something about Akar's attacks felt...*off*.

Recalling Master Maverick's lessons, most Mages had a single element in their repertoire, like fire. Dual element wielders like Lucian were rarer than rare. If anyone were to have all four elements, it would've been Aaron but certainly *not* Elias. And even stranger yet, the entire time that they fought against Akar, he couldn't sense where Seraphina and Rosalie were.

"Aaron, you still have some mana left, right?" Lucian asked, as silently as possible.

Aaron slightly nodded his head.

"I need you to summon a few more of your Lychnuses and steal Akar's scepter at all costs. Hopefully, they'll be able to retrieve your sword as well."

"What are you planning to do?" Aaron asked, preparing to follow Lucian's lead.

"You know what they always say," Lucian quoted. "Pride comes before the fall."

Luckily for Lucian and Aaron, Akar's attacks weren't strong enough to fully overpower them. Lucian signaled Aaron with his eyes, and they commenced the second stage of their plan. Aaron managed to muster enough energy to summon three more Lychnuses: One to steal the scepter, one to retrieve the sword, and one to distract the evil god.

Covered in Aerus's barrier, Lucian barreled toward Akar, seemingly reckless. Swinging his sword, Ignis clashed against Phantom. Upon contact, Lucian moved out of the way, creating space for one of the Lychnuses to gain a clear path to the sword. With its mouth wide open, the Lychnus speedily and aggressively tore Phantom away from Akar's hand.

Lucian expected to see some form of reaction, but Akar seemed unfazed, unfortunately. In the same manner, Lucian lured Akar's attention away from his scepter, and the other Lychnus tried to snatch it. The same trick didn't work twice, unfortunately. Akar summoned a fireball that burned the Lychnus to a crisp. The third Lychnus suffered the same fate.

Fortunately, Aaron appeared at Lucian's side with the Phantom sword in hand. Although Aaron looked worn out, he radiated an unbreakable resolve. Due to his advanced skills as a swordsman, Aaron taunted Akar, purposefully missing Akar's face by a hair.

"Two against one isn't fair, you know?" Akar said, in a not-so-serious tone.

With Aaron back in action, Lucian focused on separating Akar's soul from Elias's body.

"Why don't we just kill him?" Aaron suggested. "A soul without a living vessel will surely have to leave the corpse at some point."

"We can't kill him," Lucian said, sternly. "Elias was cruel and a bully, but he doesn't deserve to die because of Akar."

"Wasn't he the person who sent you here in the first place?" Aaron asked. "Why are you so adamant about avoiding any sacrifices?"

"Because they're not necessary. Leave Elias to me. Try and figure out where Seraphina and Rosalie went. My intuition is telling me that something's wrong."

"If I sense that you're in danger," Aaron said, "then I'll end Elias's life, whether you like it or not."

Going their separate ways, Lucian watched as Aaron summoned a creature that Lucian had never seen before. He didn't have time to examine it closely, but out of the corner of his eye, the creature seemed strangely familiar. The fluffy tail, especially, reminded him of someone...

Coming face-to-face with Akar, Lucian looked past the god, hoping to see the teenager, whose soul had been submerged into the recesses of darkness. Elias's soul had to be trapped somewhere. However, if his soul had already given up, then all hope would be lost to save him from his inevitable fate: a painful death by Aaron's sword.

Defensively blocking Akar's attacks, Lucian started openly taunting him by saying, "Hey, Elias, how does it feel to know that Akar chose me over you? How does it feel to know that everyone who adored you is dead? Tell me the truth, did Emilia ever truly love you, or was she simply too scared to refuse you?"

"Your pathetic words fall on deaf ears," Akar said. "Nothing you say to him will affect him anymore. Just give up, so he can finally be free from his pain. All you have to do is become my vessel, and he'll perish in peace."

"Not a chance, Akar. Lucian retorted. "Your peace *is* pain."

Seeing a slight opening, Lucian lunged his sword at Akar.

The opening abruptly closed, and Akar swung his scepter at Lucian's head.

Lucian reacted and ducked below Akar's sight line.

Repeating Akar's words in his head, Lucian devised a devious plan. *Nothing I say, huh? Well, here goes nothing!*

Wrapping his hands around Akar's waist, Lucian pulled down Elias's pants, exposing his undergarments. Although, on the surface, this act was nothing more than a harmless prank, it held a deeper meaning for Elias and Lucian, as Elias and his goons often subjected Lucian to this same humiliation on many occasions. Although Akar, a god, wouldn't be affected by mortal emotions like shame and embarrassment, Lucian knew how the prideful and narcissistic Elias would take such a slight. And that wouldn't be to sit in silence.

After evading several more attacks, Lucian stared at Akar, watching for any slight change.

"Foolish mortal, that won't—"

A crack in Akar's cocky smile revealed an enraged Elias surfacing from the depth of his soul. His cheeks turned a bright red as he yelled profanities at Lucian. For the first time ever, Lucian was glad to see his angry-as-a-bull bully. While Elias's soul was fighting for control, Lucian snatched the scepter out of Elias's right hand and retreated to safety.

Elias's soul sadly wasn't strong enough to expel Akar entirely. The ancient god was steadily regaining full control over Elias's body. Knowing that the same tactics wouldn't work twice, Lucian did what he had to do. He snapped Akar's scepter in two.

At the precise moment that the scepter snapped, the illusionary barrier broke around them. While Aaron's search seemingly bore no fruit, the broken scepter had done the trick: The black fog surrounding them faded away.

Returning to reality, Lucian noticed Akar's vessel, Elias, was quickly deteriorating. That barrier, Lucian had surmised, was a fake world meant to stall the vessel's decay and to separate Seraphina and Rosalie from Lucian and Aaron. The stone heart resting on Lucian's neck started to burn. He glanced over at Aaron, who was also grabbing at his neck and showing a look of discomfort. The faster Elias approached death, the hotter the stones burned.

"I won't let you win..." Akar seethed, blood spilling from his vessel's nostrils.

"It's over, Akar," Lucian and Aaron said together, as they approached him with their swords held at the ready. "You've already lost."

"Even if I lose this body," Akar maniacally proclaimed, "I need only to steal one of yours!"

Escaping from Elias's body, Akar's soul surfaced. As

quickly as his soul could travel, he first tried to enter Lucian's body. Unfortunately for Akar, Lucian's body was covered in Aerus's barrier. As an extra precaution, Morpheus's soul reacted, covering Lucian in his black flames.

"It's now or never!" Lucian yelled at Aaron.

Each of them grasped the stone hearts in their hands and called on the name of Veritas.

But nothing happened.

"Why aren't these stupid stones working!?" Lucian cried out in frustration. "We made a blood pact, Veritas! Fulfill your end of the deal!"

Looking like a lost ghost, Akar sourly said, "You mortals always seek us gods to do your bidding. Even now, you're relying on a god to end your fight."

"Shut your mouth!" Lucian swiped at the floating soul. "Veritas proposed the deal, not me, you stupid soul!"

"You only have yourselves to blame for the stone hearts not working, child," a familiar voice said.

In front of him stood Titania.

"Titania, what are you doing here?" Lucian asked, confused by her sudden appearance.

"Aaron summoned me," Titania succinctly said. "You refused to call on me as your Familiar, so I took things into my own paws."

Aaron continued by saying, "The stone hearts are

solely shadows of the real hearts that govern the gates between The Three Realms. Titania told me that the stones are the original El Stones, which store the living, beating hearts of Morpheus and Adonis. As we are their Reincarnates, our hearts must be aligned to open the gates and call upon the gods."

Akar, who floated as a wandering soul, said, "If I can't have you, Lucian, then I'll settle for Damian instead!"

Like in Lucian's case, Akar's soul sprang at Aaron but was repelled. Aerus had extended his reach and layered his protective barrier over Aaron, too.

"Even if you manage to defeat me, you're not coming out of this fight without any consequences," Akar bitterly said, gesturing toward Seraphina.

Lucian and Aaron turned to look at Seraphina, whose body lay still on the ground a fair distance away. Rosalie hovered over Seraphina's fallen figure, holding a sword, poised to strike. Even if they sprinted, neither Lucian nor Aaron could've spanned that distance to save her in time. Rosalie's hand rose for the final blow, plunging her sword down with a mighty force.

At that moment, the hearts of Aaron and Lucian, the Reincarnates of Adonis and Morpheus, aligned. Between the two of them, they could hear each other's internal voices screaming their companion's name, *"Seraphina!"*

Flashes of light filled the sky, the gates between The Three Realms, opening all of them at once. Akar, in his soul form, was snatched instantly into The Heavenly Realm. Despite the flashes of light and Lucian and Aaron successfully defeating Akar, their eyes were fixed solely on the horrific scene playing out before them. While the gates had successfully opened and Rosalie was released from Akar's control, it was too late. The damage had already been done...

Regaining her senses a second too late, Rosalie's blade stabbed directly into human flesh. But it wasn't Serphina's flesh... The blade pierced an unexpected substitute, who jumped in between Rosalie and Seraphina, acting as a human meat shield. Collapsing on top of Seraphina with the blade wedged in his back, Elias let out a bloodcurdling cry.

Lucian and Aaron raced to the scene.

Carefully lifting the bloodied Elias off Seraphina, Lucian cradled Elias's head in his arms. Even though Lucian still held some hatred for Elias in his heart, he couldn't fathom why Elias would've sacrificed himself for someone else. This entire sequence of events didn't make sense.

"Why did you do that?" Lucian asked, befuddled.

The light fading from his eyes, Elias stared up at the

overcast sky and said, "I let them die...Emilia...James...Peter...my family...I thought I was leading everyone to glory. My foolishness led them to their deaths, instead."

Even as Elias slowly descended into eternal sleep, Lucian kept repeating the words, "Don't give up. Help is on the way."

"Thank you, Lucian," Elias said, as his voice grew softer by the second. "I'm sorry...I really...am."

Elias rested his eyes, falling into an eternal night.

During this time, the sun stayed hidden behind the clouds. Releasing the last bit of dirt above Elias's makeshift grave, Lucian, Aaron, Seraphina, and Rosalie said their prayers to the deceased. With no flowers to decorate the grave and no priest to recite the elegy, Seraphina sang a sullen song to send Elias's soul off to The Fallen Realm.

Even though the three of them had won the war against Akar, the fight left a bitter aftertaste in Lucian's mouth. He realized this war was neither a game nor a battle between good and evil. It was about the right of mankind to have a future, regardless of how imperfect.

With everything over, Lucian had finally conquered his fear of death and awakened repressed emotions from his childhood. Tears of relief, sorrow, and regret streamed down his face, seemingly not ceasing even as many minutes passed.

While the gates had split the sky apart, the stone hearts cracked into two pieces, and the red-and-blue lights faded from them. While the sun moved from behind the clouds, the souls of the ancient gods were released from their curses. Morpheus, Adonis, Titania, and the other gods and goddesses left their Reincarnates' bodies and floated upward.

As a final farewell, the piece of Morpheus's soul said to Lucian, "Surely, if the stars align, then we shall meet again, my successor." Each of the other gods said their goodbyes to their respective Reincarnates: Aaron, Seraphina, and Rosalie. Just as if they had never been in The Earthly Realm in the first place, Morpheus and the other souls ascended to the sky and disappeared into the infinite ocean of blue.

Sending them off with a smile, Lucian's heart couldn't help but hurt. Reacting to Rosalie's sniffling, Lucian turned to look at her. He saw a single soul hovering over her body, hugging Rosalie from behind. A nostalgic silver light emanated from the figure, who whispered into Rosalie's ears. While Rosalie seemed oblivious to the familiar presence, Lucian knew the soul's identity all too well.

Approaching Rosalie, Lucian thanked the soul with a soft smile and said, "Thank you for fulfilling your promise to me..."

The cold expression that she wore in life melted away into the warmest smile after death. The love for her daughter and the promise to Lucian had tied her to The Earthly Realm. The silver light shone even brighter with his acknowledgment of her efforts.

"...Melinda."

Seeing that Rosalie was safe, Melinda's soul released Rosalie from her embrace. As a human, her soul descended to The Fallen Realm, where she would return to the cycle of souls.

Rosalie cocked her head to the side in confusion as she asked, "Lucian, why did you say my mother's name? Is she here with us?"

Shaking his head, Lucian said, with teary eyes, "Melinda's soul has returned to The Fallen Realm, but she protected you all along—even after death—even as a soul."

Rosalie's sniffling turned into wailing, and Lucian hugged her tightly. Moved by the siblings' emotions, Aaron and Seraphina joined their hugging session. Crying turned to giggling as they felt relief and joy for their hard-fought victory.

After the swell of emotions lessened, Lucian said these final words to his friends and family, "Thank you for fighting with me to the end, Aaron and Seraphina. Truly, I thank the gods for protecting us and bringing Rosalie back to me. And now, I think it's time we return to the one place where we all belong...*home*.

EPILOGUE

·┄┄┄••◆ *Solaris* ◆••┄┄┄•

•────·《 *Several Years Later* 》·────•

Two unopened letters sat on the mahogany desk. Using a letter opener, Lucian picked up the bulkier envelope and slid the blade across the sticky seal. Once opened, he read the message in-depth, not wanting to miss out on any important information or timely updates regarding his friends.

The letter read:

> Dearest Lucian,
>
> I pray that you are faring well. Per my last letter, The Academy recently opened its

doors to twenty-five newly enrolled students. While this number of attendees may seem minor compared to The Academy in its glory days, we are making steady progress in informing the citizens about the imperative nature of magic and sorcery education. Little by little, we are also correcting the false stereotypes and resolving the historical conflicts between Mages and Sorcerers. In addition, I continue to train under Master Maverick regarding my future role as the Magus of Avrith. I recently received my invitation to Aaron's coronation ceremony, which I am certain you will attend. I am looking forward to seeing you, as I have missed you. I pray that you and Rosalie will have safe travels to The Terras Empire.

With Love,

Seraphina Alastair.

Lucian's lips lifted to a small smile. He had also missed Seraphina.

He then reached for the second envelope. It appeared to be a formal invitation, as on the backside of the envelope, there was the Imperial Seal of The Terras Empire. Carefully removing the wax seal, he unfolded the piece of paper with interest. His excitement was to be expected. Three years passed since he had last seen Seraphina and Aaron in person.

The letter read:

> To the Hero of Gaia, Lucian Roux,
> The Terras Empire would like to formally invite you to the coronation ceremony that will be held for Crown Prince Damian Marlais at the start of The Spring Festival. Crown Prince Damian has informed us that you share a birthday. As such, a separate celebration will be held on the following day. Since you are a special guest, you will stand with Crown Prince Damian when he is crowned as the new Emperor of The Terras Empire. If you have any questions or if there were any delays in this invitation, please do not hesitate to notify us by letter or messenger at any time. We look forward to your attendance.
>
> Signed,
> The Imperial Secretary of The Terras Empire.

Receiving two letters in one day was a special occasion. Leaving the letters on the desk, Lucian rose from his seat. Grabbing his cloak and sword, he left his rented room.

After exiting the Adventurer's Inn, Lucian headed to the marketplace, where he happily meandered until Rosalie's training session with the Lunarian Royal Knights was finished. Random citizens watched him as he walked. Unlike the strange stares he had received in Korakk, the Lunarians gazed upon him fondly. Lucian had finally found his *home*.

Heading toward a street vendor, he ordered a meat-and-veggie skewer with a mystery sauce spread on the surface. Gobbling the morsel down, his stomach thanked him with a gurgle. After some time, Rosalie joined him, showing him her calloused palms, almost as if she was trying to boast about her hard work and resilience. He patted her on the head like when she was a little girl, and she teasingly smacked his hand away.

"I'm not a child anymore, Lucian," she said, puffing out her cheeks like a chipmunk. "So, stop treating me like one before I lose my temper."

"Whatever you say, Rosalie," Lucian said, shrugging his shoulders. "By the way, I received an Imperial Invitation to The Terras Empire for Aaron's coronation ceremony. Just asking to make sure, do you want to join me on the journey early or travel there after you've finished your training?"

As they walked down the street, Rosalie stretched out her sore arms. "Training?" She laughed at him. "It's more like a mandatory lesson for *them*, not *me*. It's no wonder they lost so badly to Akar's minions many years ago."

"Don't mock them," Lucian said, sternly. "You know who they were up against. Normal people don't stand a chance against ancient gods."

Redirecting the conversation, she responded, "Yes, I'll travel with you. After all, it's no fun racing through The Wastelands on the backs of Venaris by myself. Besides, didn't you say you wanted to visit Korakk to see this Barren fellow if you ever had the opportunity?"

"Ah, Barren, right..." Lucian scratched his head, slightly embarrassed that he had forgotten about his comrade. "Korakk is an interesting place, so we should definitely visit."

Right as they were about to reach the Guild, Rosalie reminded Lucian by saying, "The King of Lunaris sent a summons for you today at three o'clock."

"What time is it now?"

Heading inside the closest shop, Lucian checked the clock on the main wall. He clicked his tongue in annoyance. "Why didn't you tell me that sooner, Rosalie? Surely, you could've at least left me a note?"

Rolling her eyes, she said, "I told you several times before I left this morning."

Laughing off his mistake, he apologized and said, "Yeah, that's right. Sorry, Rosalie."

"No dinner for you tonight," Rosalie said, flatly.

With slumped shoulders, Lucian sluggishly walked down the street.

After a few minutes, Lucian's mood lifted, as he *was* interested in the king's summons. Since Lucian and Rosalie were living in The Kingdom of Lunaris's capital city, Solaris, it only took Lucian about fifteen minutes to reach the front gates of The Lunarian Palace.

Since Lucian frequented the palace quite often, the knight guarding the gates opened them upon seeing him. Heading through the gate and strolling down the main road to the palace's entrance, Lucian admired the scenery. As Lunaris was known as The Kingdom of Light, everything from the streets to the skies shone brightly.

Eventually, Lucian reached the front doors. Another guard acknowledged him and opened them. No matter how many times he visited The Lunarian Palace, Lucian was still in awe of the architecture. Unlike The Terrasian Palace, The Lunarian Palace was coated in diamonds and other shimmering gemstones. Rows of white marble pillars lined the outer hallways, and white marble statues lined the inner hallways. From top to bottom, the palace shone in a light much brighter than its darker counterpart.

Greeted by The Royal Secretary of The Kingdom of Lunaris, Lucian was guided down the main marble-floor hallway leading to The Throne Room. A ball of stress formed at the bottom of his stomach, as he ran through the possible problems that he might encounter.

I haven't skipped my royal lessons too many times... Did I?

"It's nice to see you, Hero of Gaia, S-Class Adventurer, Royal Knight, Crown Prince Lucian Roux," The Royal Secretary, Sir Philip, said in a blatantly sarcastic tone.

"Sir Philip," Lucian started to say, "I know that I told you *not* to call me the Crown Prince, but these titles are becoming more and more ridiculous. Besides, the king doesn't mind that I've delayed my decision. Whether I stay as an adventurer or train to become the next heir to the throne, it's a choice that I ultimately must make for myself. Only you seem to stand in opposition to my requests and my will."

Entirely ignoring him, Sir Philip said, "I would advise you not to refer to King Joseph as such, or else you and I will both have to sit in an hour-long lecture regarding your royal lineage through the line of former Crown Princess Lucille."

"I know...I know..."

Resigning to his fate, Lucian followed Sir Philip and entered The Throne Room. As soon as they passed through the double doors, King Joseph merrily exclaimed, "Why, if it isn't my favorite grandchild, Lucian! Come in, come in."

More like your only one...

Approaching the throne closer than any vassal dared, Lucian bent his body and balanced on his knee atop the carpeted floor. "King Joseph, I was made aware of your summons. How may I serve you, my liege?"

"You are neither a knight nor a vassal, my boy," King Joseph said. "Raise your head and give your old grandfather a big hug."

Every time Lucian met with King Joseph, Lucian was doted on to an unprecedented level. According to Sir Philip, King Joseph managed to find out about Lucian's abusive upbringing in Caelum and made it his life's mission to heal Lucian's painful past. The level of attention and care that he received reminded him of Eteria and Ignis, who had both returned to The Heavenly Realm. Now, only memories of them remained.

"Alright, Grandfather, can you please enlighten me on why I was summoned here today?"

Stroking his fluffy white beard, King Joseph said, "Is it wrong for a grandfather to want to see his grandson before he leaves for another nation?"

Frail and old, he says... Says the man who defeated a whole swarm of Lychnuses by himself at seventy-three-years old.

"Are you planning to go out on yet another one of your expeditions?" Lucian asked.

"Not me," King Joseph said with a smile.

With a raised brow, Lucian cautiously responded, "Me?—Well then, I'll at least hear what you have to say, but no promises."

Breathing out a sigh, King Joseph explained, "My scouts stationed at the border of The Dark Lands have gone missing. I'm hiring you—not as my grandson, The Crown Prince of Lunaris, but rather as Lucian Roux, the hero who saved The Earthly Realm—to investigate."

"Flattery won't work on me," Lucian said, playfully crossing his arms. "However, you had me at the mention of The Dark Lands. When do I need to depart?"

TO BE CONTINUED IN...

AUTHOR'S NOTE

For new readers, this revelation may come as a shock, but *Among the Fallen* and *Among the Risen* were originally one novel! Without boring you too much with the details, I will say that my writing style was a little too much to fit into one novel... Regardless, I am extremely pleased with the whole process. During this eight-year-long journey, I was able to not only refine my characters but also grow as an author. Since these two books are my first set of publications, I simply hope that they brightened your day and gave you a laugh. Do not fret! *Among the Risen* is not the end but rather the beginning of a new adventure for Lucian Roux and his friends.

See you soon,
    Makena Song

ABOUT THE AUTHOR

Makena Song was adopted from Seoul, South Korea, and was raised in Longwood, Florida. From an early age, Makena's mother, Tina Song, read countless books to her, including: *The Tale of Despereaux*, *The Shadow Children Series*, and *The Missing Series*. Reading allowed Makena to let her imagination run free, as these magical scenes played out in her head.

When she was introduced to Wattpad in middle school, she gained a creative outlet to express her countless story ideas. By the time she was in high school, this vault of random ideas turned into a set of fantasy novels. After she graduated Summa Cum Laude from Furman University, Makena pursued not only a full-time writing career as a marketing copywriter but also a dream to publish *Among the Fallen* and *Among the Risen*.

Website: www.makenasong.com
Instagram: @makenasong